OWL ABOUT YULE

OWL STAR WITCH MYSTERIES BOOK 5

LEANNE LEEDS

Owl About Yule
Paperback - 978-1-950505-58-6
Published by Badchen Publishing
14125 W State Highway 29
Suite B-203 119
Liberty Hill, TX 78642 USA

For permissions contact: info@badchenpublishing.com

CONTENTS

OWL ABOUT YULE

CHAPTER ONE

The paper I unrolled wasn't really a paper. It was a brownish parchment. "It looks like an old document," I said to my sister as she gazed over my shoulder. "It has a wax seal on it and everything." I held it up. "Look."

"That's the seal of Dionysus," Archie, my companion owl, informed us as he skittered across the counter to get a closer look at the newly arrived parchment dropped—ironically—by an owl on our back porch. His white breast feathers flapped slightly when he moved. "Well, no, not Dionysus himself." The owl craned his neck forward and blinked his wide eyes. "The Zagreus, to be more specific."

"The who—what now?" Ayla asked, walking into the kitchen.

"The Zagreus," Archie repeated without explaining.

"But what is that?"

The owl craned his neck forward and blinked his wide eyes.

"What? Don't give me that look."

"The Zagreus is Dionysus's original form and myth, Ayla," my mother called from the dining room just off the kitchen. "He was the son of Hades and Persephone and worshiped by the Orphic as a resurrected god."

Ami frowned. "I thought Dionysus was Zeus's son? Not Hades."

"As Dionysus, yes," Mom called back. "But as Zagreus, he is the son of Hades." She paused. "Don't you girls remember your mythology lessons?"

"Who could remember all this? This is why I don't study the gods," Ayla muttered. "Dude has, like, a hundred names." She turned. "So, what does it say?"

I shrugged. "The parchment? No idea. I think it's in Greek."

"Bring it in here, Astra," Mom said with a hint of frustration. "It's probably just an invitation to some Dionysia celebration. Christmas, Hanukkah, Yule, Dionysia, Omisaka. December is a world of holidays in a short period. It's a wonder anyone gets anything done this time of year at all."

Well, I wasn't going to get anything done this week, I thought as I handed my mother the scroll. Only fun and relaxation and not caring about anything important. It was the first day of my first vacation, and I had a grand plan to do precisely nothing for one solid week.

I should clarify—in the human world, they have these things called vacation days. Days where a job pays you to do absolutely nothing. You don't even have to come in. The Ministry in Paranormopolis where I used to work as a fugitive witch tracker? Those sticks-in-the-mud never had vacation days.

Maybe the Witches' Council did deserve to be overthrown.

Because vacation days? They were awesome.

The detective I work with, Emma Sullivan, took her vacation days the same week I did. It all made sense. Emma is an excellent detective, but she had become overly reliant on my psychometry to help her close cases in recent months. (If you're unfamiliar with psychometry,

4 | LEANNE LEEDS

it's a witchy ability that allows you to psychically view someone or something's past by touching an object. It's a handy skill to have as a detective, especially when looking for clues.)

So, right. I'm not a detective. I'm a psychic consultant.

Emma's the detective.

But it turns out that I have a knack for resolving cases. It doesn't matter what she gives me—criminal or otherwise—we can figure it out together. And she has an uncanny ability to always assign me cases in which I can't help but become involved.

Not this time, though.

This time, I would do nothing.

For a whole week.

"Oh, dear," Mom sighed, a worried expression on her face.

"What is it?"

"Dionysus's panther, Pantera. She's been stolen." Mom looked up and blew her bangs out of her face with a huff. "Who would steal an oversized panther?"

My youngest sister, thirteen years old, burst out laughing. "The guy's a god, and he couldn't come up with a more creative name for his panther than Pantera?" Ayla asked, astonished.

"Pantera literally just means panther in Latin. Like, literally. It would be like Athena naming Archie Noctua. Totally redundant."

"Oh, please," Althea, fifteen, told Ayla with a smirk on her face. "Like anyone knows Latin these days."

"Is there anything we need to do about this missing panther?" I asked my mother, bracing for an answer that would not be conducive to the supposed rest and relaxation I was supposed to be getting this week. "I, um, have some time."

"No, I don't think so," Mom said. "Dion sent it to me in case I knew anything, no doubt." She grabbed her fork and then paused it, hovering over the scrambled eggs. "It's also possible he was so drunk when dictating these scrolls that this one came to us by mistake." Mom speared a chunk of egg.

"Do they get along?" I asked (not believing either existed).

"Athena and Dion?" Mom asked, surprised. "Of course. It's Hera that's a problem." Mom shuddered. "Although Athena and Hera are friendly enough, you don't want to end up at the same cocktail hour as Dion and Hera. Goodness. That would be a disaster."

* * *

"Do THEY GET ALONG?" Archie mimicked, after breakfast. The owl perched on branches I'd placed in the corner of my mini-apartment attic for him. "You don't believe in the gods. So why even ask the question?" Archie ruffled his feathers in irritation. "You know, you insult your mother's beliefs every time you ask a disingenuous question like that."

"Hold up, there, Mr. Judgment. I'm not insulting anyone by participating in a conversation, Archie." I drew the comforter loosely over my bed and threw the decorative pillows back on haphazardly. "Free will, remember? That's what you told me when you showed up claiming to be a gift from a goddess. That I had free will not to believe."

"You know, your free will is starting to chap my tail feathers," he grumbled and then made clicking noises—a sound he only made when agitated. "Your friend Godfree Carrillo hiked through the entire twilight realm to stick his head through an aurora and tell you what's what." He jerked forward with his wings spread out. "You believe in Guru Bernie of Cassandra, but not Athena?"

"I can see Guru Bernie," I responded with a shrug. "With my own two eyes."

Archie responded with the sweetest growl ever uttered by an animal.

Running footsteps pounded the stairs to my attic just then. (I should probably set aside some time during my vacation to frame and build a door.) As I moved toward the clean, folded laundry, Ayla came in. "What are you doing this week?" she asked excitedly. Then, without waiting for an answer, she added, "If you go to Cassandra, can I come so I can see Melvin? Please?"

My sister, raised in relative isolation by my mother, made a new friend on Halloween. She'd worked with me on a case involving Cassandra mediums, Paranormopolis witches, and ghosts—the ghosts were the main reason she came along. In any case, Melvin Platt was the person she remembered most from the experience.

He was a friendly enough kid.

His father was a bit tough to take, though.

"Leave Astra alone for five minutes, squirt!" Althea called up the stairs. Footsteps again, and another sister entered into my obviously un-private apartment. "Let her get her laundry done and take a breather." Thea smiled at me. "I folded it for you. Consider it a vacation present."

"Are you two bothering Astra?" Ami called up from the second floor. Her steps pounded the stairwell, and she dashed up to my room.

Seriously?

"Ayla's trying to get her to…" Althea started to explain the begging campaign, but then she looked at me and thought better of it. "She's trying to get Astra to say 'yes' to going to Cassandra this week."

"Because she's trying to see Melvin?" Ami asked with a speculative glance at Ayla. Althea smirked knowingly. "Melvin can come to Forkbridge, too, you know."

"Not the same," Ayla sulked. "I'm always in Forkbridge. I want to be somewhere else. Besides, there are so many ghosts to talk to in Cassandra!"

"Okay, okay," Ami exclaimed, putting her hands on her hips. "Let Astra decide what she's going to do this week. You made your request clear, and we need to open Athena's Garden. It's just a week before Christmas. The shop is super busy, especially now that we have some high-end pieces from Aurora's Jewelry in Cassandra. Okay? Promise?" She stepped back down to the second floor after waiting for our two youngest sisters to nod.

Althea rolled her eyes, and Ayla stuck her tongue out.

"She acts more like Mom every day," Ayla muttered.

"Are all three of you working this week?" I asked, my eyebrow raised.

"Yeah," Althea said while pouring jerky steak strips into Archie's bowl. "You haven't been here for Christmas in years, but it's not like what you remember. We get swamped."

"A lot of people give New Age and witch stuff as gifts for Christmas. It doesn't make any sense to me at all, but they do," Ayla explained. She approached the double window and gazed out. Then she gave me a wave and pointed down the street. "See? People are already lining up."

"It gets a lot worse this week," Thea told me. "When Christmas falls on a weekend day like it does this year, we're slammed the whole week. Like, the whole week." Thea frowned. "Ugh. My hands are going to be all cracked from all the potion mixing I'll have to do."

"You want I should poop on them?" Archie asked in all seriousness.

"My hands?" Althea asked, startled. She drew

her hands back and quickly stuffed them into her pockets.

"No, the people downstairs."

"No, Archie. Hey, do you guys need help?" I asked, my hope for vacation sinking.

Althea's eyes widened, and she vigorously shook her head. "You're on vacation. Mom and Aunt Gwennie told us not to ask you for anything this week." Althea glared at Ayla. "But some people clearly don't want to follow the rules."

"I wasn't asking for her to go out of her way!" Ayla told Thea, her cheeks flushing. "If she happens to be going to Cassandra, and it happens to be after the shop is closed, I asked her if she would take me along! That's all! I wasn't breaking any rules." Her eyes narrowed dangerously. "Don't you dare go tattle on me to Mom when I didn't do anything."

"Look," I said, aware that I was probably committing myself to an evening trip with Ayla, "I haven't talked to Emma yet, but I do know she mentioned wanting to see the Christmas light display in Cassandra. So, since that only happens at night for obvious reasons, we will probably head over there sometime this week."

"And I can go?" Ayla asked excitedly.

"I said we will probably go. If you don't get

grounded for smarting off to Mom, and if you don't get grounded for doing something unthinking, maybe you can come with us. If we go. I'll talk to Emma, but she likes you. I suspect she'll be fine bringing you along."

Ayla squealed with joy.

"I'll try to talk to Emma about making a Cassandra trip this week," I told everyone. "But Ayla—if she says no, she says no. I can't promise anything."

I offered to assist my sisters in opening the shop, but Thea said she and Ayla would be fine. "Besides, you have chores you need to do, too, before you get to start your official vacation," she reminded me and then glanced at the laundry.

"Right." I nodded.

"So, anyway…" Thea looked at me for a long time.

Wide-eyed.

With an expectant look on her face.

"Look, I don't even know if we're going, how many people are going." My brow furrowed into its usual sardonic position. "I'll let you know, okay?"

Althea sighed but nodded. Ayla had already forgotten about the tentativeness of the plans.

She was back at the window, counting the waiting cars with a frown.

* * *

EMMA and I sat on a park bench, enjoying the usually mild Florida winter weather. "So," she said in an anxious voice. "What do you aspire to do with your vacation time? We have a total of five days. There are seven if you include the weekend."

I turned and looked at her with concern. "You appear to be stressed. I don't believe you're supposed to sound stressed while on vacation." I heard myself, of all people, telling her to relax.

"I'm not stressed. I'm shocked. We're actually on vacation. I didn't think it was possible." She sighed. "Okay, maybe I'm a little stressed. We're just sitting here on a park bench. Doing nothing. I can't help it. It's unnatural."

"You don't like to relax," I said.

She laughed. "Tell me something I don't know. I always feel like I'm wasting time if I'm not doing something. I wouldn't mind sitting on this bench for hours if we were staking someone out, right? But just to sit here? And do nothing?"

It was like a category five hurricane that had stopped at a rest shelter.

I could understand her nervous energy. Emma was always busting her butt, working hard to get everything done. She was a quick study, sharp— even with a vampire brother, she'd jumped into all the unfamiliar paranormal weirdness going on right under her nose like she'd been born to it.

But she couldn't relax.

Every spare moment of her life was spent doing something to keep herself busy, learn more, or improve her investigative skills, anything to avoid being stuck in one place in stillness and quiet.

Of course, it takes one to know one.

"What about a spa day?" I asked.

She shook her head. "I'm not much for pampering."

"A short Caribbean cruise?"

She stared at me. "You want to pay money to sit on a big boat and drive around in a tiny, itty bitty little cabin with only a circle in the wall to look out of?"

"They have a deck, you know. Or we could pay for a suite with a balcony."

"Meh." She shrugged her shoulders and looked out at the children playing. The children ran, then stopped, then ran again in an endless cycle. Emma looked envious of them, all clustered around a dilapidated park bench while imagining themselves on a grand adventure.

I changed tactics. "How did you ever get the courage to join the military or to take the detective's exam when you won't even get a pedicure?" There we go. Insult her gallantry. Make it seem like an act of bravery to face overindulgence. "Take a chance, for goodness sake."

She laughed, and the laugh was a map of her inner nervous system, a mix of care and disquiet and confusion. "One has nothing to do with the other. And besides, not wanting to go on a cruise or take a spa day makes perfect sense to me. They both involve being pampered. I don't like it. Being pampered," She sighed again.

"Okay," I said. "We'll have to think of something else. How about off-roading on the beach? Mudding?"

"For what?" she asked. "We drive in mud all the time."

"For goodness sake, Emma, we need to do something."

"Like what?"

I wanted to punch her in the nose.

"I don't know, Emma. That's why I'm suggesting things." I was breathing heavily in and out through my nose to calm the frustration. "You tell me, then. You hate all my suggestions. What do you like to do that doesn't involve sitting still?"

She put her hands under her chin. "You know, Astra, I really don't know. I've never had the time before to just do what I want. First, I was in the military. Then I was busting my butt to make detective. Then I was busting it again, trying to keep my rank even though no one wanted me to have it. So I've never thought about it."

My phone buzzed. "Well, think about it." I pulled out my phone to read the text. "We can't sit around all week and waste all this time. We won't get another vacation until next year, and we live in a place with so many tourist traps it would take us a year to visit them all." I glanced at the screen. "Oh, come on."

"What?" Emma slid over on the bench and looked down.

ORPHIC SHOWED UP. SAID HE SENT SCROLL. SAID DIONYSUS THINKS ATHENA STOLE PANTERA AND ORPHIC HELPED. WANTS MOM TO HELP HIM FIND PANTERA. SINCE ATHENA STOLE.

My phone buzzed once more after a brief pause.

SAID DION WOULD KILL HIM AND FIGHT WITH ATHENA.

Emma stared. "Someone stole a heavy metal band from Texas?"

I shook my head. "Supposedly, it's a divine panther."

"Who's Orphic?" Emma asked, squinting.

"Not a who, a what. An Orphic is a priest of Dionysus."

"Is your Mom a Thenic, then?"

I raised my head and looked at her. "No."

"Just a question, resting thunder face," Emma responded with amusement. She sat up straight, her eyes wide open as a paranormal problem rolled into her field of vision, drawing her attention away from the thought of getting a pedicure. "So, if Dionysus is a god, why doesn't he just go find the missing panther himself? I mean, he's a god, right? You'd think they'd be pretty good at knowing all, right? Isn't omnipotence their thing?"

"Probably because he—like all the other gods—doesn't exist," I told her, slipping my phone back in my pocket. The sun warmed my face as I raised my eyes to the sky. Then, after a few moments, I sighed. "The problem is the priesthoods of these mythological idiots do exist."

"Isn't your family a priesthood of a mythological idiot?" I shot her a look. "I'm just saying. They're just people, though, right?"

"Well, witches," I said. "And if the Orphic priests think the Athenian priestesses stole their stupid panther, my family might be in danger. The mythical make-believe god might be a nutty drunkard that sleeps with everything that moves, but his followers are a bunch of guys that abstain from meat, wine, and sex."

"Well, they seem disciplined."

"Right. They also study and chant about drunken debauchery and bacchanals every day." I stood up. "As you can imagine, they're a little tightly wound—and I've met a couple. Not the brightest bulbs. Most couldn't pour water out of a boot with instructions on the heel."

"Got it. Well, we have to go find this panther, then," Emma said, jumping up.

I glared at her. "Try not to look so excited."

"I'm not," she said, shaking her head with a wide smile. "I'm so disappointed. This is terrible. Awful. It's ruining our vacation." She started a steady march toward the parking lot. "Should I bring the Malibu, or should we take your Jeep?"

CHAPTER TWO

*E*mma was almost giddy as I opened the door to Arden House.

"I thought you were different!" shouted a male voice I didn't recognize. "I thought you would stand for what's right. But you're like the others, aren't you? You're like the rest of Athena's followers. You're corrupt. Bloated, pompous perfectionists tainted by your god's arrogance!"

Well, this didn't sound like it was going well.

"I'm sorry, Alexarchos," my mom said, sounding frustrated. "Our relationship with Athena is not the same as your relationship with Dionysus. She doesn't tell us when and where she goes. I can't just order her to come here. But I am certain—absolutely certain—that she would never catnap Dion's panther."

Emma and I entered the kitchen to find my mother and aunt sitting at the table while a pale, black-haired man in his early twenties paced back and forth like a tiger. He had both ears pierced, both nostrils pierced, and his entire body appeared to be a canvas for various tattoos.

"Got Ami's message that we had a visitor," I told my mother. "Hello, visitor." I extended my hand. "Great tattoos."

Mom and Aunt Gwennie smiled at me.

Alexarchos ignored me.

"You're Athena's high priestess, and you'd have me believe you have no knowledge of what she did," Alexarchos said, his voice shaking with anger. He stopped and stared down at her, his fists balled tightly. "I'm not a moron. There are rumors a panther was spotted in the temple of your goddess. If it didn't come from you, how would it get there? Everyone's entitled to act stupid once in a while, but you, Priestess, really abused the privilege."

"Okay!" I jumped in before my mother smote the arrogant little jerk.

He tilted his head in my direction without looking at me. "What do you want?"

Rude.

"How about you calm down," I suggested with a pasted-on smile I didn't quite feel. I'd hoped to be knee-deep into a massage right about now, not trying to keep some goth Orphic from insulting my mother. "No one here's got a problem with you, but you keep pacing like a lion near a wounded gazelle and tossing insults like they're arrows, we will."

My mother stayed silent, watching.

"And who are you, exactly?" Alexarchos turned to face me, a rage etched into his features. "Why should I bother answering your—" He came to a complete stop, looked me in the eyes, and then his face turned white beneath his sparkling facial jewelry. "You're a Ministry fugitive tracker!" It was clear that he was beginning to panic as he looked to the right and then the left. His voice rose an octave. "Dionysus would never ask for the Witches' Council's help! Never!"

"Buddy, there is no Witches' Council anymore. No Ministry, either," I told him. He stared at me like I'd grown a dragon head out of my shoulder. "I work for the Forkbridge Police Department." I pointed toward Emma. "That's Detective Sullivan. She's human. I'm Astra Arden, the high priestess's daughter. I'm a witch." I nodded at Mom. "We're"—I pointed back and forth to Emma and myself—"on vacation. So imagine my extreme unhappiness when I got a text that someone was back at my house yelling at my mother."

He laughed angrily. "But you're wearing the uniform! Who would do that?"

"Did the guy with earrings in his nose on both sides, two ears pierced, and almost no available skin for a new tattoo just comment on my fashion choices?" I asked Emma.

"Yup," she responded. Then she smiled.

I couldn't help but feel a twinge of resentment as Emma walked into this tangle of a situation and looked to be having an absolute ball. She seemed to need drama to swirl around her like a tornado to be happy—which seemed odd coming from someone who claimed to be non-dramatic.

"Look, dude, everything's changed," I explained. "For the better, or so I've been told. No one's out to get you. There's no fugitive retrieval service, Imperatorial City is now Paranormopolis, and they're trying some kumbaya thing there where every supernatural species gets a say." I waved my hand. "No one there is going to care that you lost your cat. I promise."

"It's not a cat!" he roared at me, forgetting his previous anxiety. "It's Pantera, Dionysus's favored mount! A panther as big as a horse!" He extended his hand out and pointed at my mother. "And she, or her stupid goddess, knows where she is!"

"Alexarchos, calm down," I told him again in overly distinct syllables.

The Orphics I'd met previously were kind of dimwitted. A little dull, a little boring. Not menacing, though, and they rarely got angry.

Not like this.

"Don't tell me to calm down!" He grabbed a kitchen chair and wielded it as a weapon, staring at me as if I'd just stepped through a time-space rift.

I reached out my hand and yelled, "Stop it! Put that down!"

So…

Yeah.

About that hand…

I'd intended to step forward and yank the chair from him.

What I actually did was zap him with a sizzling white beam of starlight that— unintentionally—shot from the center of my palm. The two-second starlight strike knocked him out, and the tattooed Orphic collapsed to the kitchen floor.

Snoring loudly.

* * *

"I KNOW we have to respect the Orphics and their path, but my, what an unpleasant young man that Alexarchos is," Aunt Gwennie observed with a frown. She reached out and picked up her knitting.

"He must be frightened," my mother observed quietly, her face drawn and tense. I watched with surprise as Mom got up and grabbed a pillow to place under the Orphic's pierced head. "Dionysus may be a god, but he's a capricious one. An unpredictable god can be difficult to serve. And right now, the god he serves thinks his priest betrayed him."

Emma watched her and then asked, "What do you mean?"

Mom rose from the floor and motioned toward the kitchen table. "This morning, Dionysus went out to his stable to find that Pantera, his panther, was gone. Alexarchos had been assigned to care for the panther, and

Dionysus found him asleep in a stall." Mom glanced back at the priest. "Pantera's stall, to be exact."

"Okay, forgive me for taking time to point out the obvious, but why would someone commit a crime and then take a nap at the scene of it?" Emma nodded in agreement with my conspicuous observation. "The fact that someone found Alexarchos in the panther's stall indicates that he probably didn't take it."

"And who keeps a panther in a stall?" Emma added. "Panthers can leap twenty feet vertically. I mean, a stall? You're sure he said a stall? Not a cage?"

"Pantera is no ordinary panther," Mom said. I rolled my eyes. She narrowed hers. "What? Do you have something to say, Astra?"

"Let me guess, she's a divine panther?"

"You really have to stop with the refusal to believe in the gods, dear," Aunt Gwennie reprimanded me with a look of near cartoonish astonishment. "For a while, the idea of an atheist witch from a family dedicated to Athena was sort of cute, but you're in your early thirties. Leave that kind of rebellion to your sisters. It's time for you to get with the program."

I stared at her with my mouth slightly open.

More than anyone else in my family, my aunt had always accepted my choices in life—and always encouraged me to use that freedom to choose. "Where is this coming from, Aunt Gwennie?" I asked, then glanced at Mom briefly. "This doesn't sound like you."

"You have starlight shooting out of your hands, dear," my aunt added with a shrug. "Your refusal to examine your own role in the universe as the chosen of Athena no longer appears to be a commitment to your ideals." She tilted her head down and looked at me over her glasses. "You just look stubborn. Especially after the veil message from your friend Godfree. Goodness, even a human could have processed that one by now." She raised her eyebrow. "Astra, the message was sent to you through someone with the name *Godfree.*" She sniffed. "I mean, really, child."

My mother tried to suppress a chuckle but failed.

That's kind of what I needed to tell you, Godfree had said through the veil. *That you are ready. But you're choosing not to be. You need to lead again, Astra. But before you can lead, you have to believe.*

"You know, I believe in her," Emma mentioned quietly.

"You believe in who?" I asked Emma.

She took a necklace from inside her shirt and held it up so I could see. A small medallion sat next to her cross—a blue circle that sparkled like it was full of tiny little stars. A woman holding a spear and an owl were depicted in gold at the center. "I don't worship her or anything," she continued, her voice firm. "But she's the reason you and I found each other. And something divine's been helping us along the way."

"I believe what I can see," I told them.

They looked at me expectantly.

I didn't say any more. Frankly, I shouldn't have to.

"Do you remember what that woman told the guy she was with at the aurora thing on Halloween in Cassandra?" Emma asked me. "She told him that if he believed, he would see it. That's what faith is, I think, Astra. You know? He'd see that aurora and those who'd passed on if he'd expected them to be there. He wouldn't if he didn't believe they were there."

"When did you become such a spiritualist?" I asked.

"Well, I hang around with witches all the time, and my brother's a vampire. Heck, my captain's dating a medium," Emma responded with a snarky toss of her head. "It was bound to rub off at some point."

* * *

ALEXARCHOS'S GAZE alternated between me, Emma, Mom, and Aunt Gwennie. He'd awoken, attempted to move, and appeared astounded that four women had managed to bind him so tightly to a chair. "I suppose you're going to turn me in to Dionysus now so I can be executed." He grew pale again. "Or—worse—handed to Nemesis for punishment."

"No, we're not doing any of that. We just don't want to get hit in the head with a chair," I told him. "You were a bit charged up, there, Orphic."

Alexarchos looked at me, sighed, and closed his eyes. "I apologize for the disrespect." When he reopened them, I realized Alexarchos wasn't so bad-looking. He had a square face, a cleft chin, and well-defined cheekbones. He'd be kind of attractive if he didn't dress like a Sex Pistols reject. "You're priestesses of Athena, and regardless of what she has done, I should show you some respect for that. I didn't."

I looked him over and nodded. "I'm not a priestess, so no harm, no foul. I would appreciate it if you didn't throw a chair at my mother or my aunt, though." I glanced at them. "They're older. They may not bounce back from something like that."

"Thank you, Astra," my mother said sharply without looking at me. "Why is Dionysus so sure that you assisted Athena in Pantera's disappearance, Priest?" Frowning, she added, "For that matter, why is Dionysus so sure that Athena is behind the catnapping at all?"

"Yeah, why not Hermes?" Emma asked with a shrug.

We all looked at her.

"Well, these are Greek gods, right? I've been reading about them lately because...well, it's obvious why, right? Anyway, isn't that dude the god of thieves and liars?" Emma looked at us expectantly. "Stolen cat? God of theft? I mean, that makes sense, right?"

No one answered.

"Let the paranormals talk, dear," my mother said to Emma kindly—but sternly.

Emma nodded, her cheeks slightly pink. "Yes, ma'am."

The Orphic swallowed. "Zagreus believes I helped whoever kidnapped Pantera because the panther was in my care. I didn't report her gone to Dionysus." He smiled crookedly. "That I was sleeping at the time is of no consequence."

"Who's Zagreus?" Emma asked.

"Dionysus," my aunt told her.

The detective looked perplexed. "Okay. I still don't get it, though. Why accuse Athena? Or, by extension, Astra's family?"

Alexarchos explained that Athena refused Dionysus's invitation to *Dionysia*, the god's personal December festival. The gods used to live in a cloud palace on Mount Olympus in Greece like the great stories told—but now they live in mansions all over the world. Dionysus's current residence was a Palm Beach mansion. "He has affected the culture there. Palm Beach house parties are now always hosted by a DJ called a *party god*. However, it is not always Dionysus," Alexarchos explained. "He is very proud of that."

"You know, I read about these parties in the *Palm Beach Post*," Emma said with a nod. "The police were called to break up a large party in Boynton Beach. They just walked in and threw it because the property owner was in Germany. They used the house as if it were their own and didn't have permission to be there at all." She looked at Alexarchos curiously. "The cops there say it's becoming a real problem."

"Dionysus is simply trying to encourage joy," the Orphic responded without shame.

"And why did Athena refuse to participate in the joy?" Aunt Gwennie asked.

"Oh, I can imagine," Mom murmured disapprovingly.

"She replied that using someone else's home without permission was neither just nor wise, even in the pursuit of joy." Alexarchos swallowed and dropped his eyes. "And that if Dionysus continued to 'borrow' people's homes without permission, that she would 'borrow' something he valued. To show him how it felt."

"The panther," I guessed.

"Athena did not say, and I did not ask for more information than Dionysus was willing to shout at me," Alexarchos responded, wincing. "Athena is majestic and stern—even her brother Ares fears her." He looked up with tears in his eyes. "But surely my death is not just. If she knew I was being cast out or executed for her lesson, she would intervene, wouldn't she?"

"The ways of gods are not the ways of witches or men," Aunt Gwennie told the defeated Alexarchos with a mysterious expression. "We can't say whether she would or would not. We do not speak for our goddess in the same way that you do for your god."

I felt like I'd walked off the set of *Buffy the Vampire Slayer* and onto the set of *Xena: Warrior Princess*.

The Orphic dropped his head, his eyes cast downward. "I know I have no right to ask after I burst in here the way I did, but will you help me?" He raised his head. His ice-blue eyes did not blink as he stared at me. "Please, chosen one. I throw myself on your mercy."

I sighed. "Look, Alex—"

"Of course we'll help you," Emma blurted out without asking any of us if volunteering to help Edward Scissor-nose over here was a good idea. "It will be tough to accomplish if we are unable to visit the stable in Palm Beach. Of course, you're assuming Athena stole the panther, but there's no proof, right? Just that letter scolding Dionysus." She looked at me. "Do you think your starlight stuff will get us into the stable if we don't take him? We can either sneak in or do something else. Dionysus, after all, sneaks into homes and throws parties all the time. I don't think he'd call the cops."

"You know, this isn't a murder-mystery game with Greek gods as characters," I told her sternly.

"You can't just jump into the middle of something like this. Let's say—for argument's sake—these really are the Greek gods of old running around the United States throwing house parties." I put my hands on my hips. "Ever heard the story of Arachne? Medusa?"

"Yeah, but I thought you didn't believe in the gods," Emma said wryly.

"Oh, I don't know what I believe anymore," I responded in frustration, waving her teasing away like it was a buzzing bee. "That guy sitting right there? He's real. The panther is probably real, too. The house parties with borrowed mansions? Those are real—and I've read those articles, too." I stared at her. "They've had shootings there."

"Ooh, you think?" Emma asked. Her hand went immediately to her sidearm.

"You *really* are hopeless."

"Oh, man, you gotta lighten up, Astra." She pointed at Alexarchos. "He's afraid of something, and if he goes to the cops and tells them the story he just told us, they'll laugh at him. Then he'll be locked up in a psych ward." She stepped closer. "He has no one else to turn to for assistance, Astra. He is unable to go to the cops. You said in your supernatural world, there are no cops or the equivalent right now. So tell me, who else is going to help out here? What other options does he have?"

With frustration, the cynic inside me banged its head against an imaginary wall as I wavered, leaning first one way, then the other. Emma, as endearing as she was, had a valid point. We'd be leaving Alexarchos with nowhere to go if we didn't help. But, on the other hand, we had no idea what we were getting ourselves into if we did help.

And, of course, I didn't want to get involved.

I wanted to be on a beach with cabana boys bringing me drinks.

"Mom?" I asked, turning toward her. "What do you think?"

My mother considered the young man—still tied up on our kitchen chair, a pitiful expression on his post-punk face—for a brief moment. Finally, she nodded. "We are here as a temple of Athena, a place people come to for help." She looked at me. "He has asked for our help."

I stepped forward to untie the Orphic. He paused before looking at me. When Alexarchos finally met my eyes, his expression was grateful. "Thank you. The panther is a part of me. She is truly everything to me."

"Don't thank me yet," I replied. "We've never done anything like this before. Panthers, gods, Palm Beach," I added as the ropes dropped to the floor. "We have no idea what we're in for."

"Yeah, but we got this," Emma told him, grinning widely.

CHAPTER THREE

"So, you know, I think it would be helpful —for the sake of argument, at least," Emma said as we drove down the coast toward Palm Beach, "if you just accepted the idea of some being named Athena with, like, unexplained powers. Don't think of her as a god if it makes you uncomfortable."

I looked out my window and tried to ignore her. I didn't want to argue about this. I just wanted to find the panther fast and then find a masseuse.

Forkbridge was north of Orlando, and Palm Beach was north of Miami on the state's east coast. I was impressed. We'd gotten all the way to Vero Beach without anyone harassing me for my religious beliefs (or, more to the point, my lack of religious beliefs).

And by anyone, I mean Emma.

Until now.

"Do you want to get off at 60 and find someplace to eat for lunch?" I directed Emma's attention to the approaching exit sign, giving her plenty of time to change lanes and head for it— and giving her plenty of time to refocus her attention on food. Instead, she sped past the exit and continued south on 95 without answering. "Okay, then. I'm going to take that as a no."

"There's a place in Port Saint Lucie that has the best trifle ever," Emma responded as she passed a slow Cadillac with a silver-haired driver. "I mean, we are technically on vacation, right?" She glanced over at me. "No reason we can't treat ourselves to a fancy lunch while we check out Palm Beach."

"Sounds good." My mouth watered at the thought of a creamy, custard-based dessert dripping over a layer cake and topped with berries and toasted almonds.

A passing motorist honked his horn and Emma glanced toward the back seat, irritation clouding her face for a millisecond before she put on her best fake smile and waved at him.

Suddenly, she slapped the steering wheel. "Actually, I don't think they're open for lunch. They're dinner only. Darn it."

So much for the trifle. "Emma, I don't care where we eat."

"You sure?" She glanced over at me. "What do you think? A burger and fries? Or maybe something more exotic? Maybe a gyro? A Cuban sandwich?"

"I mean it. I don't care."

Okay, I sort of cared.

I rolled down the window and gazed up at the sky, hoping to see Archie. Despite the arrival of an Orphic priest on our doorstep, the goddess's very own owl never came by to see what was going on. If Athena was a goddess and did exist, you'd think she'd send her owl to investigate the situation. If Archie was truly Athena's owl. "I'm just hungry, that's all," I said distractedly.

"Why am I more excited about this than you are? We're going to look for a supernatural panther. Heck, even if it winds up being *just* a panther—I mean, that's a cool case. A stolen panther, Astra. When's the last time you looked for a stolen panther?" She snapped her fingers. "You've never looked for a stolen panther. Have you?"

"You're more excited than I am because it's something new and different, and you have a paranormal fetish at this point," I said somewhat insultingly. "I'd think that after what happened with your brother, you'd be less interested in magic, gods, and the supernatural, but you keep coming back for more."

"Wow, the snarky bug really crawled up your butt this morning." Emma cast a pointed glance over at me, clearly indicating that if she could get out of the conversation, she would. Unfortunately, the two of us were locked in this car with my dark mood. "Look, I get it. You're in your early thirties. You don't want your mom telling you what to believe, and now your favorite aunt is climbing on that bandwagon. I mean, I have to deal with my mom at Thanksgiving. She's constantly up my butt about getting married. So I get it."

"Yeah, why aren't you married yet?"

"Don't you start." She pointed. "Hamburgers? At least it's not a chain."

"Fine."

* * *

"PALM BEACH IS ACTUALLY AN ISLAND?" I asked Emma as we crossed the intracoastal waterway. "I didn't know that."

"Well, the rich people don't want to let just anyone in. Gotta have a moat around the castle, you know." Emma let out a sigh and turned to face the road ahead. It was congested, and a long line of cars waited for a light to change. "Year-round, this place has a population of roughly 10,000 people, but November through April? The island is stuffed with the wealthiest of the wealthy. Population goes up to 25,000. At least."

"That's a heck of a change," I said as we crawled forward.

"Palm Beach, home of Donald Trump and former home of Jeffrey Epstein," Emma pointed out with an eyebrow raise. "I wonder where Dionysus would fall on the corruption scale between those two."

"Corruption?"

Emma gave me a look that suggested a complex answer to my one-word question, but she chose not to respond. "We should probably find a hotel if we're going to stay here a couple of days."

"Are we?" I asked her. She looked at me. "Going to stay here a couple of days? We don't even know if Dionysus will talk to us, let alone whether we'll be able to enter the property to inspect the stable at all."

"Well, you're the one that's been grousing about this case ruining our vacation. We're in Palm Beach—the playground of the mega-rich and uber-wealthy. Home of more than thirty billionaires. The 27th wealthiest place in the United States, according to Bloomberg. You know only 4.1% of jobs in this place are held by people that actually live here? If you wanted to visit a testament to wealth and excess, you couldn't do much better than a trip to Palm Beach."

"What are you, a Florida tour guide?"

"Palm Beach is one of those weird places that just screams money," Emma explained as she exited the congested highway onto local roads. "A long strip of an island holding dozens of mansions that could be converted into hotels at the drop of a hat; they're that big." She laughed. "In fact, I think that's what Trump did. Convert his—"

"Can we *not* talk about Donald Trump?" I asked. Emma and I developed a friendship without ever discussing national politics. I was hoping to keep it that way.

"Ooh, what if *he's* Dionysus," Emma teased. "Well, I mean, he could be."

I shook my head. "He can't be. He doesn't drink alcohol."

"Huh. Good point."

She drove past a spectacular home, and I couldn't help but gawk at it. The stunning residence was followed quickly by another even grander house. Palm Beach was like a candy shop for architecture and design. "Sorry, I got distracted. What were you saying?"

"It's easy to get distracted," she admitted. "Palm Beach is gorgeous. And I was talking about Palm Beach and how everything is big and expensive here." Emma drove up to a police station and parked halfway between a strip mall and the station's front door. She took out her phone and sent a text message to someone. "One of the guys I served with in Afghanistan works on the force here. He knows we're coming."

Nodding, I asked, "What did you tell him?"

"Nothing about Greek gods, magical panthers, or Orphic priests," Emma conceded. "I just told him we had a case in Forkbridge that might tie into the house parties being thrown down here, and I wanted to ask him about them. That's all. Nothing crazy." She looked up. "There he is."

Standing tall and heavy with beautiful honey skin, this man exuded an aura of masculine power as he scanned the parking lot for Emma's car.

I swallowed.

Wow.

He positively radiated dangerous energy. His hair was short, thick, and black, and it was unstyled—as if he knew he already looked good enough without using a brush. He pushed the door open and slid into the backseat, his gaze locked on Emma.

"Hello," he said, his voice as smooth and rich as velvet. He beamed a thousand-watt smile, revealing a dazzling set of pearly whites. "It's great to see you, Emma."

"How've you been, Eddie?" She extended her hand to me without waiting for an answer. "This is Astra Arden, my kind of partner, Eddie." I turned around and offered the detective my gloved hand. He moved forward slowly and deliberately, his deep light brown eyes analyzing me. "Astra works for the police department as a psychic consultant."

"Edgardo Renzo," he responded, his deep voice slightly accented with a Spanish tinge I couldn't quite place. After we shook, Eddie withdrew his hand, passing it just close enough to my exposed shoulder that his pinky brushed against my skin deliberately. It was so brief an image *almost* flashed in my mind, but the contact was gone before it could form. "My friends call me Eddie."

"What should I call you, then?" I joked.

"Is there a reason I shouldn't consider you a friend, Ms. Arden?" Detective Renzo asked me. His voice was devoid of emotion, but his simple statement conveyed the impression that whatever I said next would significantly affect our interactions.

I said nothing.

Renzo returned to Emma as if sensing I wouldn't respond. "There's not much going on here today, and my captain told me I could help you unless I'm needed for a more pressing issue." He smiled, revealing his teeth in a way that was both sexy and a little menacing. "Perhaps we can head over to Palm Lodge Coffee. They have tables overlooking the beach." He glanced at me. "The story of these house parties?" He sighed. "It's a more complicated one than it should be."

"Why is it complicated?" I asked him.

"Oh, this is not official," Eddie Renzo said, a flicker of irritation crossing his face. "The official story is this is entirely *un*complicated. According to the Palm Beach Police Department, all of this is a result of young people seeking to have a good time wherever they can. Teenagers from the eastern part of the county who are bored. I'm sure you can appreciate their desire to simplify the story for the media, right? It's not, in fact, simple at all." He sighed and waved his hand. "I'm sorry. I'm a little frustrated. Let's meet at the coffee shop. I will tell you what I know." And without further ado, he slid over to the door, hesitated for a moment, and then exited the car.

Eddie Renzo has interesting energy, I thought as I watched him walk back into the department building. I reached up and rubbed my shoulder.

Very interesting energy.

"Isn't he awesome?" Emma asked me.

Well, he's something.

* * *

DETECTIVE RENZO STRUCK a pensive pose as he waited in line as if pondering something far more complicated than the coffee orders he had to repeat to the cheerful barista. As Emma and I waited for him to return, I cautiously shared my thoughts with her. "He's got kind of intense energy. Is he always this serious?"

As if he heard me, he looked over at us from across the cafe and smiled.

"Okay, he heard me," I told Emma.

Emma raised one hand in a wave when she found Eddie in the distance. Once more, he bowed his head and returned his gaze toward the counter. "Is that your psychic sense, or you just accusing the guy of something because you're super suspicious, and you assign weird supernatural motives to everything everybody does?"

"Me?" I laughed. "I think you're projecting. I didn't accuse him of anything. I made an observation, and I asked a question. That's all."

Running into a paranormal at your local coffee shop or on your local police force would have been the most unlikely of scenarios ten years ago. The previous rulers of the supernatural world, the Witches' Council, simply would not have allowed it. Only witches could live in the human world, and only if they made sure no one discovered what they were.

And, if they did, the consequences?

Someone like me would come and get them and drag them away to be punished.

Anyway, one polite civil war later, and those old rules no longer applied.

That might be a good thing—I didn't know yet. The problem, though, was that no one could agree on the new rules. Last I heard, they formed a committee to study the idea of a committee in charge of forming committees to study proposed laws. Or something.

"He saw some stuff in Afghanistan, you know?" Emma continued, her voice low. "I mean, we all did, right? If you want the truth, it was war and wasn't exactly the most organized of wars. Half the time, we weren't sure why we were doing what we were doing or what the objective was," she admitted, trying to look less upset about her statement than I knew she was.

"No, I get it. But honestly, it seems more than that."

"He always reminded me of a wolf," Emma told me in a conspiratorial whisper. "But it could just be his hair. I'm always tempted to run my fingers through it. As if he were a big, shaggy puppy." Her cheeks pinked, and she looked down shyly.

My jaw dropped. "You're attracted to him."

"Well, duh." She looked at me like I was nuts. "You're not?"

"No, I mean, you're *attracted* to him. You *like* him."

She cleared her throat and looked up, looking me right in the eye. "Well, of course, I do. He's a good friend, and we went through a lot together over there."

"I don't mean that, and you know it, Emma Sullivan."

"Just shut up," she snapped, spotting Detective Renzo walking toward our table with a tray and three coffee cups. "We can talk about it later. But don't say anything." Her eyes narrowed. "Promise me."

I nodded just as Detective Handsome slipped back into his chair—and handed Emma her coffee with a wide, knowing smile. "Just the way you like it," he said in that rich baritone. "It's just missing the desert sand."

"I can do without that, thanks. Anyway, you know what I like?" She grabbed the coffee. "Info. Come on, Eddie, spill it. What makes these house parties so complicated? In your opinion."

Eddie took a sip of his coffee and stared out of the window. "I suppose the pleasantries had to end eventually, yes? Okay, I will tell you, but I have to start at the very beginning. You'll see why in a minute."

Detective Renzo arrived in Palm Beach immediately after his military service and quickly rose through the ranks thanks to a knack for arresting and detaining suspects with no injuries —apparently unheard of. "My bosses were impressed, but I was just fast," he said, shrugging. "Good cardio. Strong."

I was surprised he did not thump his chest to illustrate.

As a reward (after he passed the exam), Eddie was promoted to detective when another detective was fired after an investigation into a fatal shooting. "Almost immediately," he admitted, "the house parties started."

Eddie thought the group was well-organized because they could identify the largest mansions along the coast that were also empty with no one on the grounds to stop burglaries or report intruders. "They knew the day—the very day—a maid would unexpectedly have the day off, or a security guard called in sick. What's more, they knew *in advance*." Again, Eddie's eyes searched my face for a reaction. "They could plan, announce— even if the situation didn't seem to be knowable in advance."

"An inside job?" I asked. "Maybe the

unknowable absence is nothing more than a low-level employee getting a payoff."

"I thought of that, looked into it. There was nothing that indicated that. Nothing that," said Eddie, pausing to sip his coffee, "demonstrated any were at all involved. No money changed hands; nothing in their lives changed. On the contrary, they claimed many times to not know themselves they would be gone that day."

"That's bizarre," Emma said.

"Or a huge conspiracy," I pointed out.

The door to the coffee shop opened and a little old lady walked in. A hostess greeted her and escorted her to a seat on the opposite side of the large room.

"I have been working on this for months," Eddie told me, his finger pounding on the table. "For months, Ms. Arden. There isn't a single shred of evidence pointing to a conspiracy between Palm Beach's maids and security guards. These are people who have spent their entire lives working here."

"After a lifetime of working, maybe they're tired of being worked too hard or paid too little." I looked at Emma to see how she reacted to his story. Her head was cocked toward Eddie, her eyes wide with curiosity. "I mean, what you said is weird but not unexplainable."

"They knew the combination to the various safes," Eddie argued, pushing back and staring at me. "They knew exactly what to steal and when to steal it. No one who attends the parties knows who invited them or informed them that the party was taking place. There are so many people that even if we raid one, the people responsible are long gone, and the items stolen are long gone before the raid even begins."

Emma looked at her friend and then looked back at me. "So, it's a theft ring, really, that throws parties to cover the crime and confuse the police?"

An elderly lady slammed into the back of my chair with such force and weight I was thrown forward. Eddie Renzo instinctively reached up with his large hand and grabbed my shoulder to keep me from hitting the table.

Images flashed through my mind in an instant. Memory flashes, disjointed images— running through a forest. A large moon rises above the water. Cloth ripping, a view of the beach, and then a closer look at the beach before Renzo—

"Oh my god, you're a freaking werewolf!" I gasped, shrugging his paw off me.

He drew back his hand, his face expressionless, and didn't seem surprised by my statement. Eddie finally nodded once, a brief acknowledgment. "You are a witch, then," he observed quietly. "I thought as much from your uniform, but I had to know for sure."

"No." Emma's gaze flitted back and forth between us as she spoke. "No. This can't be happening." A wave of uncontrollable laughter erupted from Emma, and people three tables away looked at her to see if she was okay after the shock of it. "Everyone is a paranormal except me. You. My brother. Now Eddie. Everyone. This can't be happening." She wiped tears from her eyes. "This is so unfair."

She stood up, pushed her coffee out of the way, and stopped laughing.

I reached toward her. "Emma—"

"Don't," she warned me, turning on her heel and heading toward the coffee house's deck. "I need a minute. Just don't follow me. Either of you. I just…I just need a minute."

CHAPTER FOUR

Through the cafe's front window, I caught a glimpse of Emma. With her ankles crossed, she rested against the concrete block wall and watched the cars drive by in the parking lot. She had a defeated look on her face. "Damn," I muttered under my breath as I shifted in my seat.

"She'll be fine," Detective Renzo's calm voice reassured me.

I felt my rage build as I studied the handsome detective with a cold stare. "Look, Fido." Renzo winced almost imperceptibly. "I don't know when you talked to her last? But she's been through a lot in the past year. I have no doubt she'll be fine." I glanced back toward her. "That doesn't mean it isn't hard to process or that I'm not annoyed you put her through this at all."

"You don't like me."

I rolled my eyes and shot him a *well, duh* expression. "You could have just asked her if I was a witch instead of playing the game you did this morning," I told Renzo. "And if you really are a werewolf, you've probably heard about the Arden witches of Forkbridge, anyway." I leaned forward, my voice rising. "Sure, maybe you don't read the paper and really never saw a picture of me—and this outfit—after Emma and I solved a bunch of cases. Maybe Palm Beach doesn't care what happens in a little town like Forkbridge, three hours away, so you never had any reason to hear about it. Whatever. Don't know, don't care."

He took a drink of his coffee and gave it a little swirl before putting it down on the table. "I sense a 'but' coming," Eddie Renzo told me, his eyes shadowed.

"But the other explanation is *you* haven't talked to Emma in a long time."

"Is it?"

"Yes. Because she and I? We've been joined at the hip for most of a year. She isn't under any threat of being turned into a frog if she talks about me. You could've simply asked her." I scowled at him, trying hard not to explode. "Either you heard about me working with Emma —a woman named Arden that can read objects through her skin—and didn't bother to have an upfront conversation with your friend, or you don't really know Emma as well as you think you do anymore."

"Ms. Arden, I—"

I pushed myself forward with a jolt. "And if that's the case, *you* have no business telling *me* she's going to be all right. You should be asking me what I think. Not the other way around. Fido."

An uncomfortable silence stretched between us. A nerve jumped in Detective Renzo's jaw as his right hand gripped the side of the table.

"What?" I asked, angry. "Come at me, Fido."

The wood creaked under his weight, and a tiny squeak came from the woodwork.

Finally, Eddie Renzo looked past me with an exhale, his face fixed, his eyes carefully blank. "You know, witches aren't in charge of 'lesser' paranormals anymore," Renzo said, his voice low.

I jerked my gaze back to Renzo, meeting his eyes. "What are you even talking about? I know that. I got marched out of my home of thirteen years when it happened, dude. I know that better than you do."

Renzo nodded, looking suddenly sad. "You talk with the arrogance of the Witches' Council, calling me 'Fido' and lecturing me."

Now it was my turn to wince. "Look, I didn't mean—"

"You do realize you sounded completely patronizing, don't you?" He waited a few seconds for an answer, but I said nothing. "Especially when you act like I, a werewolf, would have no cause to be concerned about you, a witch tracker that worked for the Ministry. Like there's no reason for me to be cautious with you." He glanced toward the window. "Or with her now that she's palling around with you. Your people and mine have a history."

I glanced from the detective to the window, trying to figure out what to say next. He was studying me intently, and I could feel my back stiffen. "Fine, yes, okay, we have a history," I told him, my voice quiet. "I am not the Witches' Council. I'm sure there are things in your department you don't stand behind. Things the military did you disagreed with. The Ministry was no different."

"The Ministry was different. The Ministry killed people."

"Do you really want to argue which group's black ops were worse, here? Regardless, that's no reason for you to lie to Emma, not ask her..." I looked back at him, took in his frown. Then I exhaled in frustration. "Oh, I don't know."

The problem was I did know.

And he was right.

As long as I wore this uniform, other paranormals would see me first as a threat. My argument was ridiculous because it didn't matter who was worse. Witches oppressed...well, everyone. Every supernatural everywhere. For centuries. And I was a small part of that for thirteen years. Finally, the rush of angry adrenaline started to drain from my body.

"Sorry," I said shortly. "And sorry about the 'Fido' crack."

I tried to swallow the anger that bubbled up to the surface every time someone hurt Emma. First her brother, and now this guy. I'd been wrong, ultimately, about Rex. Maybe I should back myself up a bit and give this guy half a chance. Right now, my tearing him a new one wasn't helping Emma or the situation.

What's done was done.

"Thank you." Renzo nodded.

"Look, I didn't mean to get so angry. It's just that I noticed your repeated contact with my shoulders, the only exposed skin I have. I figured you knew exactly who and what I was when we showed up today, and the cagey crap set me on edge." I looked at him closely through narrowed eyes. "I don't like that you tried to communicate with me behind Emma's back. She's my best friend and my partner. I don't hide things from her."

"Fair enough," he said shortly once again, his dark eyes searching my face.

"You clearly know something about the case we're working on," I said, my voice a little calmer. "And you clearly don't trust me." I set my coffee cup down, feeling a tightness in my chest. "Obviously, I don't trust you. But maybe we got off on the wrong foot. How about we start over, Eddie?"

Renzo nodded, shifting slightly in his chair. "Okay, Astra." He scooped up his coffee cup and took another sip, eying me over the rim. "Let's start over."

"Besides, you might need my help in a minute," I muttered.

"Oh?"

"At some point, Emma's going to realize she's known you for years, and you never told her you were a werewolf." I sat back. "To be blunt? You might need a witch in a bulletproof bodysuit to disarm her when that revelation hits. Just saying."

* * *

"SORRY ABOUT THAT," Emma announced, sliding into her seat. "So, werewolf, huh? That's really interesting. Maybe once the case is over, you can tell me what that's like." She took a deep breath and drank, her grip becoming increasingly firm on her coffee cup. "So, Astra. Have you told him about Dionysus yet? I mean, since he's one of you."

I sat back in my chair and focused my attention on her. "Are you okay?"

Emma only managed a shaky grin for me. "I'll make it." The detective nodded, but our eyes stayed locked. "Did you tell him what we're really doing here?"

"What do you mean?" Eddie Renzo looked at me, frowning.

"I didn't say anything to him while you were enjoying some fresh air. I reasoned that it would be best to wait until we could all discuss it together." I raised my eyebrow. "You want to start?"

Emma's lips clenched. Her fingers clasped around the mug's handle. "Yeah. I'd love to talk about this later after the investigation is finished."

"Sorry, what?" I asked, confused.

"Emma, are you okay?" Emma's eyes were fixed on Detective Renzo when he posed the question. "I'm sorry I didn't tell you—"

"Ugh. No," Emma murmured, her voice cracking. "I'm not okay." She glanced back and forth between the two of us. "You don't just tell someone that someone they've known for years is a werewolf, and not expect..." Her voice trailed off. "Not expect something, anyway."

Renzo's face was filled with concern. "Emma, I—"

"Look, I'm fine," she responded sharply, her expression troubled. "I didn't mean to say that like that. I just don't want to talk about that right now. I need to focus on the case."

"Are you sure?" he asked her.

Suddenly, Emma closed her eyes, her fingers curling over the rim of her espresso cup. When she opened them again ten seconds later, she had a blank expression on her face. "Okay, so we're here because of the house parties and the break-ins," she told Renzo, her voice completely steady as if all the emotion she'd been feeling was just shoved down and out of the way. "There's more to it than what you told us, though—and considering who you are, I don't know how much you know."

"I don't understand," Renzo said, frowning.

"This morning, a pagan priest showed up on the Ardens' doorstep—"

"An Orphic priest," I corrected, using the more specific title.

Emma looked at me. "Yeah, one of those." She returned her attention to Eddie Renzo. "He claimed Dionysus's panther, Pantera, had been kidnapped by the goddess Athena. He's also been accused by Dionysus of helping her because he slept with the panther in a stable—"

"I suddenly realized how obscene that sounds," I said.

Renzo's face brightened as he realized something. "Big cats in a stable?" He pulled out his phone, jabbed at the screen, and squinted. "Peter Liber owns a gigantic waterfront property on one of the most exclusive parts of the island. The Florida Fish and Wildlife Conservation Commission has been out there several times because the guy has a permitted panther. He's not meeting the requirements."

"What are those?" I asked.

"Class I wildlife—which includes panthers obtained after 2009—can't be kept as a pet. The permit holder has to have Biological Sciences qualifications, ongoing training, and this guy seems to have a permit without any of that stuff," Renzo admitted. "Most of us figure he greased someone's palm to get it, and every time they show up to check on him, he probably just hands out cash like candy. They report to us every time they go." He looked up. "They go a lot. Nothing ever changes."

I frowned. "I don't understand. Then why do they keep investigating?"

"Liber's neighbor keeps complaining that he doesn't have the panther caged, that the animal just wanders around the property like a house cat. All permits require adherence to structural cage requirements, and he just flagrantly violates them." Eddie Renzo looked at me, a puzzled expression on his face. "Now that you mention it, I could swear I saw a report that says the guy keeps the panther in a stable."

I read off the address the Orphic priest had given us.

"Yeah, that's him."

"The Greek god Dionysus lives in Palm Beach." He laughed, but it was a nervous laugh. "That's a new one on me. Suddenly, I'm thrilled you two are here."

Emma's lips pursed together in concentration. "Well, at least Astra will be useful," she said finally.

"Emma, you're one of the most capable people I know," Detective Renzo told her, his voice gentle. "I've seen you deal with things that should have been too much for you to handle, and you not only handle it, you conquer it. You're the only person I know who could put up with finding out you were with a werewolf in a fox hole and not flip out. I mean, this? This is like..." His voice trailed off, and he looked past us, lost in thought. "I think you're taking my revelation better than I'm taking yours."

Emma's cheeks flushed. I'm talking about a full-on fire-engine red flush.

"From what we've heard, Dionysus is the one who organizes the parties," I explained to Renzo. He returned his gaze to the table. "He hosts some, and others host others. But they were all connected."

Emma nodded. "At least, that's what his priest said."

"So, what do you know about Peter Liber?" I asked Renzo.

"Like what?"

"Like, what is he? To the outside world, I mean."

Renzo regarded me. "I don't know much about him. His last name is German, I guess. The story I heard was…okay: he grew up in New York, went to a prestigious private school, and then went to New York University. He started his hedge fund right out of college and has done incredibly well for himself for a guy in his early thirties."

"What do you mean, 'his hedge fund'?" I asked.

"Well, let's just say that he funds, and it funds." He put his phone back in his pocket and leaned back in his chair, looking at Emma and me with a severe expression. "I know people have suspected he was mobbed up for a while, but if he really is Dionysus, all of that's a lie anyway, right? Just a story to cover why this rich guy no one knew appeared out of nowhere and suddenly had tons of money."

I frowned. "Why would someone that wealthy

want to steal things, though? Why would a god want to steal from rich people?"

"Prometheus *literally* stole fire for humanity," Emma pointed out.

"So some made-up story said," I countered.

"Oh, lord. Here we go with the 'there are no gods, only werewolves and elves and witches and fairies.' But gods? Oh, no. There can't be *gods*. Not gods," Emma said with an exaggerated expression of surprise. She turned to Renzo. "I think Hermes is hanging out with Dionysus, and he's probably stealing stuff."

"Wait a minute. Hermes is here, too? Here?" Renzo's expression was one of befuddlement. "In Palm Beach?"

"Hermes is not in Florida," I snapped. "Hermes is a story in an old book." I cradled my head in my hands, rubbing my palms against my temples. "Why me?" I muttered.

"Don't mind her," I heard Emma tell Eddie. "She's in the throes of intellectual stubbornness while mounting a one-woman crusade against belief in god."

"Which god?"

"Take your pick. She doesn't believe in any of them. Least of all, the one that gave her a talking owl and starlight hands to zap evil from the world." I heard Renzo chuckle. "I know, right? I love Astra, but man, she's stubborn."

They both laughed. The kind of laughter that made you feel self-conscious or inferior. I straightened my shoulders, tossed my hair back, and raised my head to face them.

"I'm sorry," Eddie Renzo said as soon as he caught my furious expression. "I didn't mean to laugh. It just seems unfathomable to me that anyone with your abilities would have no belief in anything greater than herself."

"Hey, now, wait a minute. That makes me sound kind of arrogant."

Renzo just looked back at me without saying anything.

"Thanks," I said. "You know, we said we'd start over, but we're winding up back in the same place we were before." With me not liking you. "I know what I believe, and if I happen to see something that makes me change my mind, I'm open to it."

"Starlight, Eddie," Emma whispered. "From her *hands*."

Renzo looked at me with a serious expression on his face. "The two of you really are a fascinating pair. You are way more than you are willing to admit, Astra." He turned to Emma. "And you, my old friend, seem to be devastated by the idea that you can't be more than what you are." A gentle grin came over his face as he sat back in his chair. "I bet you two came together for a reason, and are both wrong, unintentionally —in your own way."

"I'm not following you," I said.

He chuckled. "I have no doubt about that."

Emma smiled at me and nodded. "As much fun as this is—giving Astra guff for her reactionary atheism—we have to get a move on." Emma looked at Eddie. "Astra's mother is the high priestess of Athena, and her family might be in danger if Dionysus really does think Athena stole his panther."

Detective Renzo smiled and straightened his posture. "So, we investigate the panther's disappearance, and I gather what information I can on the house party theft ring situation as we go?" He was a hulking muscular guy, yet he slid out of the booth with the grace and ease of a dancer.

"If we have time," Emma said, "we can help you with that—after we get the panther back." Eddie locked his gaze on Emma's with a penetrating stare, causing her to flush once again.

Oh, lord.

I guess she got over the wolfman thing.

Suddenly, my phone vibrated. "Just give me a sec," I told them as they both made their way to the door. It was a text from Ami, and I opened it.

I KNOW UR BUSY BUT GLOW CARD FELL. NOT STAR CARD. APOLLO CARD. PICTURE WITH WOLF. MEAN ANYTHING TO U?

When Apollo was alive, he was known by various names, including the god of the Sun, healing, archery, and poetry. One of his lesser-known titles?

Wolf-god.

Great.

CHAPTER FIVE

Guilt swelled inside of me as we drove toward Peter Liber's palatial home on the coast. I looked ahead to Renzo's car in front of us and frowned.

Why *had* I called Detective Renzo 'Fido'? Was he right? Had the Ministry's intolerant attitude infected me, somehow, so I was having trouble shaking it?

I knew Renzo had been a soldier before we met. I knew he was someone Emma admired—and Emma's admiration wasn't exactly something she handed out like candy.

She'd *told* me she considered him a friend, that she respected him.

And yet, as soon as I discovered he was a werewolf, I went full-insult on him.

But it wasn't just because he was a werewolf...

Was it?

"You seem lost in thought," Emma said, glancing over at me.

"Just looking at the Christmas lights," I murmured, lying through my teeth. The rich certainly did the holiday season up with twinkling excess. There was hardly a tree—palm or otherwise—absent a deluge of decorative light abundance. Lit with tiny LED bulbs and draped in garlands of lights, even the low-hanging fronds shone like silver wreaths in the light of day. I felt like we were driving through a magical kingdom in some far-off land, and we were on our way to see its king. "The waste of electricity is kind of impressive."

"So, are werewolves bad?" Emma glanced in the rearview mirror briefly, then looked out the car window. "Is all that full-moon turning, savage attacker stuff real?"

"No, they're not bad," I told her, shifting uncomfortably. "They—like every other paranormal—are good or bad depending on the person, not the species. And there's actually nothing special about werewolves and the moon. Nothing special about wolves and the moon, either, by the way," I explained. "It's a myth, nothing more."

"So, when you say it's a myth, do you mean it's truly a myth in the sense that it's not true? Or do you mean that you, Astra Arden, have decided it's a myth until you see otherwise, and it could be true?"

I glared at her. "The moon and wolves have no relationship. Period."

"Yeah, that doesn't help me," Emma said and then sighed.

"Ami's text message before we left the cafe? A card she was using in a reading began to glow. She was using her Greek god deck, and the card she was holding was Apollo. The artwork depicts him with a wolf," I told her, changing the subject. "She thinks it might be a star card that's not a star card."

"Huh. Maybe we should start calling them glow cards," Emma said. "So what does that mean? The god Apollo is somehow involved in all this, too?"

"I think it means Detective Renzo might be in danger." We pulled up next to an open-air van with a caroling choir dressed in Colonial garb. The ladies in bonnets appeared to melt beneath all the clothes as they sang "O Holy Night." "Archie will most likely appear and provide us with additional information."

"Can he fly this far?" Emma asked, sounding concerned.

"Some owls can fly forty-five miles an hour if they have to."

"That still put him hours out, yet," Emma said as the car passed a minivan with heavily tinted windows. She drummed her index finger on the steering wheel. "You don't seem particularly worried about it."

"I'm not—your friend is an ex-soldier, a current detective, and a werewolf. I feel like he can take care of himself until Archie gets here and we get a better idea of what's going on."

Emma nodded and steered the car to catch up with Renzo. "So, I don't mean to question your witchy wisdom here, but if he can take care of himself, why do you think the card has to do with him?" Emma asked after a few moments.

A wolf card turning up within an hour of Eddie Renzo's werewolf revelation seemed far too coincidental to dismiss, and the case (if you could call it that) we were on was riddled with divine claims. Apollo interjecting himself into the situation appeared plausible—if there was an Apollo. Since there wasn't, I figured it had to be the wolf. "It just feels like it," I explained. "To be honest, I'm not sure what the two of them— Athena and Apollo—have in common to make any other guess."

"Well, Zeus fathered them both, so they're brother and sister," Emma told me, showing off her new knowledge of the Olympians. "Neither one of them is *particularly* understanding when someone crosses them, so there's that. Oh— Apollo created the Oracle of Delphi, too, so they both have some history helping humans. And that means he's connected to divination, right?" I shrugged. "So maybe he heard about you, and it's Apollo that thinks Eddie needs some protection?"

I frowned. "You think Apollo—the god who cursed women who refused his romantic advances—knows who I am? Jeez, I hope not."

"Let's be honest, all the gods had a major issue with consent, Astra."

I turned and looked at Emma. "So, what's the story now? I'm a rent-a-witch? Whenever the Olympians need something done in Florida, they toss a glowing card at Ami?"

"You know, heroes worked with a lot of

different gods in the myths," Emma said as we pulled up to a huge, golden gate behind Renzo.

"Are you calling me a hero?"

"If the myth fits."

* * *

WE WERE ALLOWED onto the property with little fanfare, much to my surprise. The gated entrance led to a sprawling expanse of manicured grass surrounded by leafy trees and manicured hedges. As we drove down the long driveway, we came across an ostrich that looked at us with interest.

"Wouldn't a free-roaming panther eat that bird?" I murmured.

The driveway widened and circled in front of a massive mansion. As I got out of the car, I noticed a swimming pool to my right, flanked by several gazebos, a putting green, and a multi-car garage full of expensive vehicles.

"This place must cost the GDP of a small country," Emma said quietly, pointing to a group of people on cushioned benches laughing around a gas-lit fire. The seating area was surrounded by Greek-style statuary in a circle. The gentle ocean waves lapped a shore I couldn't see on the other side of the house in rhythmic, drowsy repetition.

As I returned my gaze to the gate, the werewolf took the lead.

"My name is Detective Renzo and—"

"Pardon me, sir," a voice from behind me said, dismissing Detective Renzo. "Astra Arden?" When I turned around, a tall man dressed in a suit, shirt, and tie stood at the top of the front stairway, staring at us. Well, at me. "You're Astra Arden. That outfit is unmistakable, even if not one-of-a-kind."

"Okay, not strange at all," Emma noted quietly. She cast a glance at Renzo. "Did you call ahead and let them know we were coming?" With barely perceptible movement, he shook his head no.

I looked at the man on the stairway suspiciously. "Yes, I'm Astra Arden."

He gave a brief smile. "My name is Montgomery Birch," he said as he took a graceful step down the stairs. "I'm Mr. Liber's butler." The man gave a slight bow. "Mr. Liber has been expecting you and your companions."

"Has he now?" Detective Renzo asked.

Birch ignored him as if he wasn't even there.

Emma's worried expression was quickly replaced by a cheerful mask. "So, he'll speak with us, then?"

"Yes."

I looked at the butler. "We didn't tell him we were coming. So, how do you know he's willing to talk to us?"

"Quite right, but even so," Birch answered without answering.

Montgomery Birch was a pale, attractive man with broad shoulders and coiffed black hair. Despite no discernible accent, his speech patterns were clipped and almost British.

"What do you think?" I asked the other two.

"LEOs have been in and out of here dozens of times," Detective Renzo told me, his back to Birch. "I don't think we're in any danger. Besides, my partner knows where I am." He glanced back. "I think we'll be fine."

"Fantastic," the butler exclaimed as if everything had been decided. "If you'll all follow me, I'll take you to see Mr. Liber."

Montgomery turned and strolled through the large double doors into the main residence building. He stopped and looked down at us once he crossed the threshold, an expectant expression on his face.

"What in the world is going on?" Emma murmured, her fake smile still intact. "How could they have known we were on our way?" She cast a glance at Detective Renzo. "Did your partner call ahead of time?"

"No," he mumbled back, his teeth clenched. "No, I didn't call, he didn't call, and I didn't tell anyone at the station I was going to meet anyone named Astra, either."

"You know, it's a half-mile to the closed front metal gate, and if someone comes after us, we'll have a hard time getting out," I told them both. "By the way, I'm not sure your phony expressions are helping here. You two look like mannequins in the Macy's Christmas window."

Emma raised an eyebrow. "How are you remaining so unflappable in this situation?" She glanced to the right where the ostrich was eying us warily. "I hate ostriches. They always look like they're on the verge of attacking." Then, suddenly, Emma turned, her eyes wide. "Are there were-ostriches? Is that a thing? Could that be a were-ostrich?"

"Just take a breath, will you?" I said with some annoyance. I turned and stepped up to join Birch. "Let's go find out what this is all about. Maybe we can wrap it up fast and restart our vacation."

The two followed me—primarily, I suspected,

because it was in the opposite direction of the ominous-looking ostrich.

* * *

MONTGOMERY BIRCH LED the three of us through the magnificent house and out onto an imposing back patio. We took a path to the right, which led down to a large conservatory building just off the private beach. We found another outdoor living space nearby with comfortable furniture and a bar area surrounded by a flower garden.

"Get me out of here now!" Archie screeched. "She doesn't have your stupid panther, and if you don't let me out, I swear I will pelt every Lamborghini with so many owl pellets that you'll be replacing windshields from today until the next millennium rolls around!" The brass cage rattled as the wide-eyed owl flapped its wings and banged against the cold steel bars.

In the corner of the luxurious living space, in an honest-to-goodness gilded cage, was Archie.

"What are you doing here?" I asked him, shocked.

"I'm waiting for the zoo to open," Archie said sarcastically. "You idiot, I'm in a birdcage! What do you think happened? I got lost on the way to

Key West? Missed my cruise in Miami? This moron bird-napped me!"

Emma leaned into me. "I can understand him," Emma whispered.

The glowing card was real, then.

Great.

Emma could only understand Archie when we had a star card case, and her ability to understand him disappeared as soon as we did what we had to do. I glanced at Renzo. Was he the wolf on the card? I'd assumed, kind of flippantly, that he was —but now I wasn't so sure.

My heart was doing a flip-flop as I quickly tried to process the situation we'd just walked into.

"Archie, are you okay?" I asked him.

"I'm in a cage!" screamed the owl. He hissed angrily, a furious sound of rage and indignation at his captivity. "Am I in pain? No. Am I going to eat the houseboy's eyeballs with sugared spiders and spring water? That's a big 10-4, there, Astra!"

Well.

That was...descriptive.

"That's my owl," I told Birch. "Let him out." I stepped up on him. "Now."

He gazed at me with sympathetic eyes. "I'm afraid I can't do that," Birch said with another slight bow. "Mr. Liber has given strict instructions that Athena's owl is to be kept safe and secure until Pantera's return."

"He's my owl," I responded. "Not Athena's."

"Well, that's a heck of a step down," Archie grumbled, pacing his cage. "Wisest divine being in the universe to a witch that can't even—"

I whirled on him. "Do you want my help?"

Archie stopped pacing. He tilted his head ninety degrees and looked at me with wide eyes. "Fine," he said grudgingly, pulling in his wings and lowering his head. "I'm your owl. Can we go now? It's almost afternoon snack time."

Birch smiled briefly. "I can assure you that no harm will come to your owl so long as no harm comes to Pantera by Athena's hand. He'll be released when the issue is resolved."

I crossed my arms. "Yeah, that doesn't work for me."

"I doubt my master took you into consideration when making the decision, Ms. Arden, so that doesn't surprise me at all."

"Let the bird out of the cage, dude."

"I'm sorry, but no."

I crossed the patio, oblivious to Birch's polite, quiet warnings not to touch the cage. It reminded me of Archie's cage from almost a year ago, and I suppose the memory of what happened when I touched that one had faded enough that I did it again without thinking twice.

It went no better this time.

My gloved fingers had barely touched the door's lock when a wave of dizziness and nausea washed over me, the ground lurching beneath my feet.

"Astra!" Emma shouted. "Eddie, help me!"

I felt hands on me, then cushions beneath me, but the world kept spinning, spinning, spinning. Finally, I pushed someone out of the way, knelt down, and retched on the jittery painted concrete.

"Astra, what happened? Are you all right?" Emma sounded frightened. "Talk to me."

The owl frantically flapped its wings inside the gilded cage. Back and forth it went, back and forth, back and forth, thump thump thump, thump thump thump.

I moaned. "Archie, stop! My head is pounding, and you're not helping."

The thumping immediately ceased.

"Get her on the couch," Renzo said.

"I did try to warn you," Birch said with little sympathy.

"Well, you didn't try very hard, did you,

Montgomery?" a woman's voice, strong as steel, admonished the butler. "Clear her mind before Zag arrives. No woman should be forced into my husband's presence with her wits already compromised."

My thoughts became clear as soon as someone touched me on the forehead.

I looked up at a stout woman with a solemn expression on her face. Her face was soft, her lips red, but her strength was visible in every limb, in her stance, in her energy. She reminded me of a female MMA fighter with a strong build—not fat, but thick and muscular.

"Who are you?" I mumbled, still trying to regain my composure.

"Ari," she responded simply. "You and I have a lot in common, Astra," she said, smiling. "My mother was a bit overbearing as well."

I shook off my drunken state of confusion and stood up to face the woman. Standing was difficult, but I persevered. My stomach clenched against the nausea, which was gradually fading away. "But *who* are you? What is going on here, and why are you holding my owl?"

"Insurance," yelled a booming voice from the conservatory. Suddenly, music played in the previously quiet sitting area. This loud, booming techno-mix made my head hurt. "I want to reclaim my panther. I heard through the grapevine that you and your pals intend to get Pantera." The man smiled before pursing his lips. "I just want to make sure you have some incentive."

I blinked.

If Montgomery Birch exemplified elegant masculinity and Ari evidenced slightly masculine beauty, the man who emerged from the greenhouse embodied extraordinary gender-bending glamour. The man's long blond hair and smoky eyes contrasted with his bee-stung, berry-colored lips. His make-up was set off by a matching shimmering lacy blouse that opened to reveal a hairless oiled and muscled chest.

He was stunning for a man, beautiful for a woman, and amusedly looking at me.

"Are you Peter Liber?" I asked him.

His laughter was as melodic as his voice.

"Are you?"

"You really are a complete disbeliever, aren't you?" Liber asked me, his eyes sparkling with delight. "I'd heard that you were stubborn, but I thought this far into your journey, you'd be a bit more flexible." He spun around like a runway model and swooped in, invading my personal space. He laughed again as I drew back. "Flexibility is *in*, my dear, or haven't you heard?" I noticed he smelled like roses as he twirled away.

"Zag, don't toy with the witch," Ari warned her husband. "If you want her help, you'll need to be up front with her."

"Zag?" I asked, confused. "So you're not Peter Liber?"

Emma watched the exchange, her face pale.

Zag waggled his perfectly plucked eyebrows. "I have many names."

"If you want *her* help, you need *my* help, you overzealous drunken morons," Archie shouted, flapping his wings again. "Open the stupid cage door and let me out! Let me out now!"

"Hush, owl," the man said with a wave of his hand. "No one trusts you. Be nice, and I'll bring you a rabbit."

Archie, that stupid turncoat, immediately shut up and settled down.

"Will you assist my husband recovering his panther, Astra? Or persuade your patron to send Pantera back?" Ari inquired, a grin on her face like the serpent must have given Eve. "I'm not as convinced as he is that this is his sister teaching him a lesson, but we haven't found the cat. That suggests that a god has intervened in some way."

"Wait a minute, wait a minute, wait a minute. You want my help?" I crossed my arms. "I'm supposedly the chosen of Athena; you're supposedly the god Dionysus," I said, pointing toward the glorious fake. "You supposedly think that Athena stole your panther," I pointed out. "Considering all that—"

"That's a lot of suppositions," Ari observed, and then she gave Peter Liber/Zag/Dionysus a kiss. "You do, at some point, discover real facts when you investigate, yes?"

"Look, you're rich, and you're pretending to be gods, and I get all that. So whatever floats your boat, okay?" I retorted.

"Water floats our boat, just like everyone else," Peter told me with a wicked grin. "And it's not a boat, my dear. It's a yacht. A yacht is not a boat."

"I don't care."

"Then why did you bring it up?" he asked with a toss of his long hair.

I took a deep, deep breath and exhaled loudly. "Look, I don't *know* you people. We're here to investigate what happened to the panther, yeah, but only because your employee showed up—"

"Priest," the man said, fluttering his long eyelashes.

The group fell silent as we considered one another and our next moves.

Peter Liber looked at me, his stunning eyes locked on mine as if sifting through the contents of my soul beneath the sheen of rage. He finally turned to face his wife. She extended her hand. He looked at it for a moment, then nodded once.

"I'll tell you what, I'll make a deal with you," Ari smiled, stepped forward, and extended her hands toward me. "I will convince my husband to release the owl if we address your doubt first," she said simply. "If you wish to know who I am, you have only to remove your gloves and take my hands in yours."

I stepped back. "Wait, what?"

"If you wish your owl back, just take my hand." Ari stared at me, her hands outstretched. The woman's husband danced behind her to the thumping club music, a smolderingly sexy grin on his face.

I stared at her hands suspiciously. "Why?"

"So we can stop with your foolish doubting. To be frank, Astra, it's tiresome."

I looked over at Archie and raised my eyebrow.

"I've thought you were a complete idiot for doubting it all since I showed up on your doorstep, so I don't know why you're asking me like you don't know what my answer would be." Archie jerked his head to the side and shook his feathers. "Do I still get the rabbit, though?"

I stared at Ari's hands.

And then I took off my gloves.

CHAPTER SIX

"You believe now?" Ariadne, former Cretan princess, asked as I took my hands away from hers. "Did you see enough to lay down your suspicion and doubt, Astra?" Her expression was clear-eyed and knowing. The goddess helped me sit down into a chair placed behind me by Birch (in case, I suspected, I got woozy or overwhelmed at the vision).

I hadn't.

Not that it hadn't been an intense experience.

The images lasted an eternity, and the voices that spoke were in languages I didn't understand. Ariadne had lived so long and seen so much that looking into her past felt like watching a basketball game in the middle of a baseball game, surrounded by a Formula One race. It was difficult to know where to look and what to pay attention to, and I was relieved when it was over. My hands ached, and my heart pounded in my ears.

But I did see.

And I had no doubt what I saw was real.

"You were mortal once," I said with circumspection. Ariadne sat close, her perfume hugging her skin with a woody sweetness. "You weren't always a goddess. They only made you a goddess because of him." I glanced at Dionysus.

"I was mortal, once, many years ago." Her voice lowered as she sat beside me, and her face took on a solemn expression. "My grandfather was Zeus, so I was divine-touched, and the gods were much more active in the world than they are now. But yes, I know a little of how you feel, suddenly being thrust into a world of divine beings."

Emma sucked in a breath, scrolling quickly through her phone. She swiped once, then twice as the tips of her fingers flew across the screen. Finally, she looked up, her eyes wide. "That's Ariadne," she whispered. "She's the goddess of paths." She swiped once, then twice, and looked up. "Astra, did you know that when she was mortal, she was in charge of a labyrinth where sacrifices were made to Athena?" Emma squinted and scrolled. "Well, or Poseidon. People say both."

"It was Athena, and that was a very long time ago," the goddess responded, swiping at the air as if closing a curtain on a past that no longer concerned her.

"Wait a minute. It was you. You stopped the sacrifices," Eddie Renzo said, awestruck. "With... um, that guy with the ship."

Ariadne smiled, and her hand went to her chest. "Well, Theseus stopped them, and yes, we began a movement that would take years and years to come to fruition." A slight frown crossed her smiling face. "Some say, of course, that it hasn't fully died out. Even today."

"What sacrifices?" Emma asked.

"Human sacrifices, but those aren't really around anymore," Renzo said, surprised. "If they are, they're against the law."

"Didn't you just discover a dead homeless man beneath the pier the other week?" Ariadne asked Detective Renzo with a raised eyebrow. "Was he not sacrificed for the sake of profit, for greed? Someone came face to face with the man, a veteran of the military, and had the opportunity to assist him. To put him up. To take him beneath cover. To offer what they had in abundance to one who had already offered everything he had—his very life—for them. The man did not exist in isolation." Ariadne tilted her head. "That no one did offer, and he died? It was his final sacrifice, albeit one made inadvertently and without choice."

Eddie Renzo had a troubled expression on his face. He clenched his teeth and stared into her eyes with a wistful sadness.

"Don't look so sad, wolf. Gods and spirits will gather him and give what this world could not. But yes, I showed Theseus the way into the labyrinth, and I helped him get out," she said as if this happened every day. "For all the thanks I got." Her face briefly showed bitterness. "I know this isn't fair for the poor man, and it doesn't make up for life lost. But it's the way the world works. Sometimes there isn't justice or reward."

"But sometimes there is reward. If Theseus hadn't abandoned you on Naxos, my love, I might never have found you," Dionysus said and then leaned down to sweep her into his arms. He gave her a loud, smacking kiss on her forehead that brought her smile back. "My always faithful, always understanding wife."

"Yes, always faithful. Not always understanding," she murmured, her eyes narrowing. "And you would have found me. You were meant to find me."

Dionysus laughed a tremendous rolling laugh.

A laugh cut short by Emma's shocked shout of, "Are you kidding me?"

We all turned and looked at her.

"The word *clue* came from the word *clew*—as in Ariadne's *clew* of thread!" Emma pointed her finger at Ariadne. "The one she gave Theseus to guide him out of the labyrinth!" Eddie Renzo gently reached out and covered Emma's pointing finger with his hand and lowered her arm to her side. "Dude. I mean...just...dude."

"It's just a word, Emma," I pointed out. "I'm sure all words have some fantastical origin or another."

Emma Sullivan gave me a look that would have sliced me to ribbons if it had a knife's edge to it.

"Oh, here we go," Archie muttered.

Montgomery Birch walked into the greenhouse.

"Arden, I have to admit that your stoic acceptance of everything as if it were nothing is starting to irritate me," my friend said, shoving her phone back in her pocket. "You should be happy—actually happy—for once in your life! Don't you get what this means? You have proof the gods exist!" I stared without expression. "Wow. You have gone completely off the deep end into some sort of neurosis here that smothers all normal reactions if that doesn't make you—"

"Did you just call me nuts?"

Emma shrugged. "Sorry. You should be excited! If the diagnosis fits—"

"First it's my rejection of all this that annoys you. Now it's my stoic acceptance that annoys you?" I said, growing frustrated. I waved her annoyance away. "This isn't nothing. I never *said* it was nothing. But just because it's not nothing doesn't mean I've just been struck dumb by the concept of gods walking the earth and feel some desire to fall to my knees and worship these two."

Emma blinked. "Well, wait a minute. I didn't say you should. That's not what I mean. But how can you just look with your own eyes into the past and shrug it off like it was an *I Love Lucy* rerun?"

The butler returned with two metal bowls and a metal plate. He handed one bowl each to the god and goddess and placed the metal plate into

Archie's cage through a slit. The scent of roasted rabbit and buttered popcorn hit me.

"Really?" I asked him. "Popcorn? Seriously?"

"I have heard arguments with you on this topic can get...involved," Birch admitted. He leaned against the table on his elbows, legs crossed. "Please, continue. I have enough snacks to cover everyone until dinner."

I stared at him, glanced at the popcorn, and glared at Archie munching on a roasted rabbit— then turned on my heel and headed to the beach.

"Don't follow me!" I shouted over my shoulder.

* * *

THE BEACH WAS private and isolated, with only the sound of the waves breaking. I sat on the sand, scanning the foam for movement, certain that Poseidon would appear at any moment and give me his opinion on what I should do with the rest of my life.

I *never* liked religion.

Yeah, okay.

Maybe you picked up on that already.

Despite Emma's confidence this should make me happy, this didn't make me happy. Gods walking the earth, from what I read, rarely made people happy.

And, let's face it—my experience with religion wasn't the greatest.

Since I was a child, my mother's devotion to the concept of an invisible deity dictating her life and our lives irritated me. As far as I could tell, the goddess Athena did nothing for us except make my mother obsessed with people *outside* the house—and make sure my sisters and I knew we were also eternally obligated because my mother had bound herself.

Gods.

Pfft.

So, even if the gods existed, why should they have any power over my decisions? Where were they when the Witches' Council imprisoned people for opposing them? Or during the Middle Ages' Great Witch War? They sat on their buttocks and counted multi-millennium compounded cash, as far as I could tell.

They popped out sometimes to complicate things and then retreated, leaving us all to struggle through on our own.

Gods.

Pfft.

Along the horizon, I noticed a fisherman. The

boat sent wide, gleaming nets spinning out in front of them. "Follow me, and I will make you fishers of men," I murmured as I watched the men in the boat, quoting one of the world's most widely practiced and well-known religions. It was practiced by one-third of all humans on the planet.

Those fish would wind up on someone's dinner plate. So why would anyone want to follow a religious allegory that implied you should fish men?

Gods.

Pfft.

I looked down. That was one thing I didn't have to worry about, at least—that religion was meant only for humans.

Not for paranormals.

Not for me.

"You okay?" I turned to find Archie sitting next to me on the sand. "You kept your word, so Dionysus let me out. I was worried about you." He glanced back up toward the house. "That, and Emma's pelting the deities with questions. She'll remember you're down here. Eventually."

I chuckled. "You know, there are times when I think it would be easier just to be human. They're so easily amused."

Archie made a whistling sound with his beak. "You know that saying they have about the grass always being greener? Yeah, you're having one of those moments."

"I'm not, though," I told him, turning to face him. "So, up there's a goddess, right?" Archie nodded. "And she had some insight into a man—a vet—that died somewhere along this beach." Archie nodded again. "They—the two immortals up there—are both wealthy beyond most people's wildest dreams."

"Probably," Archie agreed.

"Well, why didn't she go and get him an apartment if they have power, if they move around in the world, if she knew he was in trouble? Maybe just buy him a meal? Why not use some of that money to save his life? Instead, she makes Renzo feel guilty?" I shrugged. "Just seems like a bunch of hypocritical bull to me."

Archie's round eyes stared out sideways, reflecting the glow of the sun off the waves. "I don't know, Astra. I wish I could explain to you why the gods interfere when they do and why they don't when they don't. I don't always understand, and I've been around practically forever. But I gotta tell ya—even though I've been around gods for a millennium. What you describe? That's not the way it works."

"Of course not. That's never the way it works," I muttered, grabbing a handful of rocky sand in my fist and throwing it. The quiet of the day was cut by the sound of pebbles skittering across the beach while waves washed up the shore in a wash of white foam. The coastal wind stirred my hair and blew across my skin.

"You know what a miracle is?" Archie asked me. "The humans say it's an event that is not explicable by natural or scientific laws and is, therefore, the work of a divine agency." He stepped over toward me and tapped my hands with his soft wings. "What do you think humans think of when you do what you do? They think it's a miracle, right? But we know it's not. We know there are a small number of witches left in the world, able to do things that have always been natural to some."

"So there are no miracles?" I laughed. "Thanks, Archie. If this is a pep talk, dude, you kind of suck at it."

"That's not what I just said, you dolt," he snapped and whacked me with his wing. "Try and keep up. There might be a test later. There *are* still miracles. They are few, though, and far between. The world has more capability than it ever has. They don't have to step in the way they used to. The gods don't want to *do* for you people, Astra. They want you to learn to do for *each other.*"

"Like frustrated parents?" I raised my eyebrow. "So if we can do it, and we don't do it, no god is swooping in to do it for us?"

"Something like that. Look, the gods have been around for thousands of years," Archie told me, his eyes wide and searching mine. "They have seen all of your hurt. Hurt after betrayal after hurt. Belief systems have come and gone. With each generation, humanoids and paranormals get better. Beings get better. Life gets better. But the gods, ultimately, can't do that *for* you." Archie looked off toward the ocean. "You all have to do it for yourselves for it to be real. For it to last. For your existence to matter."

Ouch.

"We're not doing an outstanding job, then," I admitted, staring at the water. As I watched, an empty plastic bottle floated onto the shore.

The gods wanted us to save the world, and we couldn't even recycle our plastic.

I didn't know why this revelation—gods exist —had made me feel so hopeless, so maudlin. Well, maybe I did—if the gods were real, we'd had consecutive pantheons of various super-powered beings wiser than we were. Yet we still, after all this time and all those lessons, hadn't figured it out?

Not a good thing.

"You have no idea how cheap life was thousands of years ago." Archie snuggled toward me and made an odd sound, like a purr. "Even just a thousand years ago. A hundred years ago. You're better. All of you. I promise. And occasionally, when the gods think you all need a little extra something-something, they send someone." He looked up at me. "You understand?"

I peeked at him out of the corner of my eye. "I'm the little extra."

"You're *a* little extra. One of many little extras, by the way—you're not witch-Jesus, so don't get cocky." Archie tilted his head. "Can you handle being a little extra? Carrying a bit of light not entirely your own? Light with a higher purpose? Using that light to make things better one person at a time?"

"I feel like you pulled a bait and switch," I told him. "This was supposed to be a job."

"It *is* a job."

"It sounds like more of a calling."

Archie chuckled. "You can only respond to a calling if you're not deaf."

I almost argued back—but a deep breath and some momentary honesty stayed my tongue. I had to admit to myself he was right.

I'd been pushing away all possibilities that this was anything other than my mother's post-military machinations. And Emma was right, too —I'd been doing it almost to the point of absurdity.

"Okay, fair point. Yeah, I can try." Archie stared at me with his round, expressive face and blinked. "What? Not good enough?"

He blinked again, fixing me with a sarcastic gaze while raising his wings slightly. "Okay, then let me be more specific—can you keep doing it, only *without* the 'there are no gods' garbage? Dial the daily blasphemy back a smidge, maybe? Remember what happened to the disbelievers in Troy?"

"They disbelieved because Apollo couldn't accept the word 'no' from a woman and cursed Cassandra, Archie," I told him, frowning at the reminder of the Apollo card. Then, before Archie could defend the misogynist wolf-god, I added, "Look, I accept Greek gods are wandering the earth. Okay? That's as far as I'm willing to go at the moment. Give me some time to process."

The bright sheen on his feathers shone along the curve of his raised wing. "Good. Then I have something to tell you."

I raised my eyebrow. "What is it?"

"I checked out the stable when I got here. Before they caught me." Archie looked down at the sand, his talons distractedly scratching a tiny ditch in it. "Athena did maybe sorta kinda take her brother's panther," he said slowly. "Maybe."

"Maybe?"

"Probably. Just to teach him a lesson."

"Probably?"

"Almost positively," the owl said with a swift nod of his bobblehead. "For sure."

CHAPTER SEVEN

I returned from the beach, Archie on my shoulder, to find the group deep in discussion about the gods on holidays. Emma wanted to know whether they—Dionysus and Ariadne—gather with gods from other cultures' religions. "Well, why wouldn't you have Odin over for a barbecue, right?" Emma asked them as they lounged on the outdoor couches. "I bet he'd make some mean ribs."

The goddess made a *tsk* noise. "Odin has his own frustrations with his followers these days. I don't know that he has time for a barbecue," Ariadne said with a crook of an eyebrow. She turned. "Welcome back, Astra. I hope the beach helped you see within yourself and process the new information you've been given."

"Yup," I responded shortly.

"So, you've gotten over yourself?" Emma asked bluntly.

Before I could answer, an earsplitting laugh exploded from the reclined Dionysus, his arm loosely around Ariadne. "I like her!" he announced to no one in particular. The god then leaned forward and gave Emma a smolderingly sexy wink. "I *like* you, girlfriend. You're brash and sassy and bold."

"You have no idea," Eddie Renzo chuckled.

"I'm sure you are brash and sassy and bold, as well, wolf," Dionysus told Detective Renzo. "I don't know why you're so quiet, watching us like we're on a stage at the Theater of *Me* in Athens. But even so. I will compliment you soon enough." Suddenly, the god looked impatient. "Give me something to compliment! Or are you a knave, here under false pretense? Your stunning good looks do not give you license to be false with me, you know!"

Well, that turned quickly.

Renzo stared back but said nothing.

"Settle down, husband," the goddess warned him. "I know well your attraction to mortals, but these have jobs to do. Pantera is still missing, and the day's sun is wearing on." Ariadne rose elegantly from the lounge and stepped around the low table in front of her. "Let's bring them to the stables so the witch can read the walls. I would very much like to know what Alexarchos did." Another slight frown. "I dislike the idea of someone we sheltered betraying us."

We walked toward another path leading away from the outdoor area. "He told us this morning he didn't do anything. In fact, it was Alexarchos that asked for our help in finding your panther, Mr. Dionysus," I told the god respectfully.

"Please, Astra, call me Zag. Especially during this time of year." The god's expression grew stormy. "That sect *stole* my holiday for their god. I mean, *I* was born of a mortal woman. *I* was fathered by a god. *I* was twice-born. Why couldn't *I* get a tree with twinkly lights and balls for cats?"

"The ornaments aren't for cats, Zag," Emma informed the god.

Dionysus stopped walking and stared, incredulous. "That's not what the cats say."

"I thought your mother was Persephone?" I asked, frowning. "She's not mortal, is she?" I looked around. "She's a goddess in the myths, right?"

Archie, still riding on my shoulder, leaned toward my head and whispered, "You maybe don't want to start asking these questions. It'll just make your head hurt, and there's sometimes no right answer."

"Nonsense, owl! The Zagreus is the son of Persephone and Hades. Yes. And I am the Zagreus," Dionysus said with enthusiasm. "But I am also Dionysus, the son of the mortal Theban princess Semele and the mighty Zeus." He smiled widely at me. "I am the twice-born, you see."

"So, you were born twice, once to Persephone and once to Semele?" Archie's talons dug painfully into my shoulder.

"No," Zag answered and then smiled. "I was born twice because Hera killed me while my mother was pregnant with me, and Zeus pulled me from the ashes." He stopped walking. "I think." He cocked his head to one side and regarded me intently. "Or maybe not. Maybe it was because I turned the pirates into dolphins. Dolphins have something to do with rebirth, right?" He stopped walking again. "Or is that trees?"

I glanced over my shoulder at Ariadne. She shrugged. "I stopped listening to his stories at least a thousand years ago. There are so many of them and so many that conflict. I often wonder if my love even knows which are real anymore."

"See?" Archie whispered.

"Well, I know which are *not* real. Euripides was a liar," Dionysus said grumpily as he started again toward the stable. "He painted me as a tortuous fiend. That? That was not my fault. It was never me, what he said. That Homer guy? He got me." He opened his arms wide and gazed out over us. "I am the comforter of mankind!"

"Yes, my love," Ariadne told him with a long-suffering sigh—as if she'd heard this all before—and gestured toward a building in the distance.

"Don't you *'yes my love'* me, woman. I am the liberator of mortals!" he said with indignation, swinging an arm out. "I am the adventurer who brings them ready-made peace and joy!"

"Yes, my love," Ariadne said again, but her expression had grown strained.

"I am the giver of wine and flowers! I don't care what Zeus says!" he cried and then paused, waiting for Ariadne to reiterate her agreement. Then, not getting it, he huffed. "I am the giver of wine and flowers!"

Ariadne turned away from her husband's snit

fit and pointed toward a large building. "Here we are."

"I am!" he yelled, his face stormy. "I am the giver of wine and flowers!"

"I love wine," Emma said, trying to appease the suddenly annoyed god.

"Flowers are fabulous," Detective Renzo added. "Just incredible. Really."

"Khloris was the Greek goddess of flowers, you know, not Wino McDrunky," Archie whispered. "But maybe don't mention that right now while he's antagonized." The owl sighed. "You see why Athena the Wise loses patience with Drunky McNarcissism over there."

"You really like your insulting nicknames, Snotty Mc...um, snotty," I whispered, not finding a good zinger to end the nickname.

Archie stared at me, his face sour. "Leave that to the professionals. You don't have a flair for it." He squeezed my shoulder. "You need a flair for it."

"Yes, yes, dear. The comforter of mankind, my love. Your wine and flowers make even the werewolves happy," Ariadne repeated sweetly, and Zag's face lit up with a satisfied smile at her soothing words. "No one remembers you putting on animal skins and running around the woods eating raw meat anymore. Not at all."

"That never happened," he murmured. "I never did that. Tabloid gossip. Fake news."

"Of course," she told him.

I watched the whole routine with some amazement.

Dionysus was funny. I had to give him that.

It was as if I had just witnessed the entire foundation of ancient worship unfold in front of me.

Divine being has Daddy issues.

Worshipers must lavish praise on divine beings as if they were girlfriends at a bar following a breakup. Then, soon enough, everyone lies to them and tells them how wonderful they are.

Divine being soaks up false praise like a sponge.

All is right with the world again—until the next temper tantrum.

"You do believe me, don't you?" he asked, his voice softening even more. "You really do believe me, right?"

"Of course, my love," Ariadne said and gently stroked his chest.

* * *

"I REMEMBER Dionysus was the god of the grape harvest, of wine, of ritual madness and celebration," I told Emma as we walked in the stable building ahead of the divine beings. "Be careful getting too cozy with him. Or believing too much of what he says."

"You've read *Alice in Wonderland?*" she asked me. I nodded. "Then you know it's a story about a girl falling through a rabbit hole into another world that makes no sense. Well, I'm no longer a girl, and this *isn't* another world. While a lot of this makes no sense, I'm still not going to randomly grab bottles that say 'drink me.' *I* have more sense than that."

I nodded and said nothing as we watched Ariadne unlock an interior door.

"So, I'm sure you have questions about what happened last night." Ariadne opened the door to a sizable angular room lined with polished wood and polished stone. It looked more like a mausoleum than a stable.

"Yes," Renzo said, his voice formal. "What did you observe?"

Ariadne's eyes swept over him, seemed to dismiss him, and focused on Emma and me.

"There are three stalls—one on the end for Alexarchos, one for Pantera, and another for storage. Pantera was never left unattended."

"So Alexarchos was either drugged, knocked out, or tired?" Emma asked.

"He said he doesn't drink, though I have my doubts." I looked at Dionysus. "Could he have been drunk?" I asked, pointing toward bottles of wine on a shelf next to the stall.

"*I* could have been drunk, certainly." Dionysus wandered over and stepped into the area Ariadne claimed belonged to the missing Pantera. "But no, not Alex. Alex is one of my priests. My priests don't drink when here."

The god glanced at his wife, who watched us all quietly. I waited for a further explanation of the rule or why the wine bottles were in the stable, but none was forthcoming. Emma and I looked at each other. I shrugged. She shrugged back.

"Got it," Emma told Dionysus in her detective's voice, pulling out her notepad. "So, why not?"

"Why do my priests not drink? Because I drink enough for all of them." Dionysus looked at Emma quizzically, as if he'd detected a sudden change in her tone and attitude toward him, but he couldn't quite understand what was different. "It's just part of the rules I lay down for them." Emma nodded but didn't respond. "What? Why are you looking at me that way? *Someone* has to be the designated driver."

"Uh-huh." Emma wrote something down and then walked around the enclosure, taking in every inch of the walls. "What about the parties you throw, again, Zag?" Emma asked without turning around.

The god's expression changed swiftly. "What parties?"

She turned and looked at the god. Her voice was gentle, but her eyes were sharp. "The ones you throw at people's homes while they're away. Without permission. The house parties."

"I don't throw them. My *priests* throw them." He suddenly gave her a ferocious stare, eyes blazing. "Wait a minute. What does this have to do with my panther getting catnapped?"

Ariadne put a hand out on Zag's arm and restrained him gently.

"You don't throw them? Houses just get borrowed and then used by your priests and"—Emma turned, her hands on her hips—"wrecked. Furniture and dishes and kitchen appliances broken, art and jewelry stolen. You knew that, right?" The stare she gave him was so intense and so unshakable that it might have been a hook sunk square into his soft underbelly.

"I don't like this anymore. Why are you looking at me like that?" he asked.

"Wonder what he thinks of her sass now," Archie whispered, still on my shoulder.

Emma slowly circled the god while she spoke. "I don't know what you mean. Like what? How am I looking at you?"

"Like *I'm* the bad guy." His voice rose. "Like I did something wrong."

The mood in the stable was becoming increasingly tension-filled.

Renzo had—wisely, in my opinion—refrained from saying much since we'd stepped onto the property of the god of wine, clearly reading the signals from Ariadne she was not interested in speaking with him.

On the other hand, Emma had built rapport with the capricious god—and was now testing those limits with her naked suspicion.

"I don't know anything about those parties beyond what I've told you," the god responded stiffly. "And I'm beginning to take offense at your words, human."

Just as the tension got thick, Emma's posture

relaxed.

"Well, Zag, I'm not trying to accuse you of anything. Just trying to help you out, right? What if your panther was kidnapped for ransom? You're a billionaire, I assume you have a lot of enemies, and you're ultimately responsible for what happens at the parties since your priests are the ones running them." Dionysus frowned at her words. "What if someone kidnapped the panther to get money from you?"

"They would never get money from me," he responded sharply. "I would never give them money."

"Fair enough, comforter of humanity," Emma responded without irony. "Are you sure they would know that?"

Dionysus frowned, which annoyingly made him just as attractive as when he smiled. "Who is 'they'? Who kidnapped Pantera?"

"Well, I don't know," Emma said, tilting her head. "Do you?"

The god first looked confused and then defensive. "She's trying to trick me," he told Ariadne, who did not respond. Finally, when his wife didn't support him, the god turned back to Emma. "You're trying to trick me," he said and raised his chin.

She was about to say something more, but I touched her. "It's enough," I whispered. "Let's take a look at what happened here first. We don't know what I'm going to see, and we might need his help."

* * *

I SAW NOTHING.

Well, not nothing.

An hour of touching various spots on the stone and wood got me little beyond a view of the panther sleeping, views of Alex cleaning the stables, snippets of conversations occurring within the building, and periodic flashes of drunken debauchery so wild I blushed.

And I was in the military.

I don't blush.

"There's a couple of explanations," I said to the assembled group as I put my gloves back on. "One is that the kidnapping wasn't that traumatic an event. Maybe it wasn't a kidnapping at all; maybe the panther just left."

"Impossible! Impossible!" Dionysus barked, glaring at me. "Pantera loves me. She would never leave me."

"Yeah, because he's so lovable," Archie muttered.

The god stiffened at the owl's appraisal. "You know, I could return you to that cage in two silent beats of your ridiculously wide wings, bird!" Dionysus shouted at the owl. "I granted you your freedom, where is your gratitude, you—"

"You put me in the stupid cage in the first place, you moron!" Archie shouted back. "You don't get points for letting me go when you were the one that captured me! What are you, an idiot? For Athena's sake, who made you a god, anyway?" Archie angrily flapped his wings. "I don't know what your problem is, but I'm guessing it's hard to pronounce."

"You impudent yard bird!"

"I've been called worse by better," Archie retorted.

"All right, that's enough," Ariadne said with a matter-of-fact tone.

"But that bird got in the last word!" Dionysus protested.

"Oh, go feed your own ego. I'm busy," Archie told him.

"I'd like to remind all of you," Ariadne interjected, raising her hand, palm out, "I am a goddess and have the ability to curse anyone in this room with a sustained thought." A ball of glowing white appeared in her hand. "This is no clew of yarn, I assure you. And I said quite clearly that was *enough*."

I felt Archie breathe in deep, and I hurried to pinch his beak together firmly. "This isn't helping," I told the owl. He glared down at me sideways over my fingers, his wide eyes fixed on mine. "Just be quiet, okay?" Archie nodded once. I released his beak, and he jumped off my shoulder and flew to the window sill.

He and Dionysus glared at each other, but they both said nothing.

Once Ariadne was assured of respectful silence, she poofed the white ball away and looked at me. "You mentioned a couple of possible explanations for why you didn't see anything about the disappearance. One was that the kidnapping was not traumatic to Pantera. What was the other?"

"That some kind of magic shielded the energy from implanting in the area."

Emma frowned. "What do you mean?"

"We had items at the Ministry that made sure any energy from an event was unrecoverable," I explained. "You couldn't scry it, read it in a reading, read it in the objects around it. It was like a vacuum cleaner that sucked all psychic evidence of an event and held it, guarded, so no one could ever see it."

"You think one of these items was used?"

"I think it's one possible explanation," I told her. "Some of the Ministry items went missing when the government takeover in Imperatorial City happened, so it's a possibility we can't ignore. The first explanation, though, is the simplest."

Ariadne nodded. "So, how do we find out which it is?"

"We investigate like we would investigate anything else," Emma told Ariadne. Renzo, standing beside her, nodded. "Though probably not precisely like everyone else." Emma looked at Renzo. "Hey—you're a werewolf. Wolves have a sense of smell one hundred times greater than humans. Do you—"

"Yes, I have a heightened sense of smell," Renzo interrupted, nodding.

"So you can scent the panther in here?" He nodded again. "Enough for us to follow her?" Once more, he nodded. "Then I think that's where we start."

CHAPTER EIGHT

"Just stay on this side," Renzo said as we walked south along the isolated public beach—or, rather, the small strip of it that was technically public. Posts in the sand denoted private ownership on the landward side of the sought-after oceanfront, each stamped with an unfriendly warning. "The locals got annoyed with people hanging out on this beach, so they marked almost all of it off." He made a motion toward the waves. "All we have to do is walk over here."

"This line appears to be extremely arbitrary," I observed. I looked up and spotted Archie sitting in the trees.

"That's the average high tide line. It becomes a set measurement we call the erosion control line," Renzo explained as we continued walking. "What's that, you ask?"

No one did.

"The erosion control line is in place to prevent private property owners from extending their land onto publicly-paid-for sand. And, to be honest, we can technically walk on that side." Renzo raised his gaze to a million-dollar estate. "The public is permitted to *traverse* the private areas. They just can't put down a blanket or chair because it's a private beach."

"It's amazing how much bureaucracy we create to control a stretch of sand," Emma said, looking beyond the private post to the large estate. "All to keep others out of our private Idaho."

Renzo stopped walking.

Emma and I stopped.

The wind off the ocean brought the scent of salt and the sound of the waves slapping against the shore. An expensively dressed couple strolled by us, hand in hand. Their bare feet kicked up divots in the sand.

The pair looked at us suspiciously, as if they were familiar with everyone who had a right to be on this stretch of beach and knew we were strangers. Before they could say anything, Renzo flashed his badge.

The relief on their face was a little bit offensive.

"Do you have something?" I questioned the werewolf after the wealthy couple had resumed their afternoon stroll. Emma turned to face Renzo, who cut a dashing figure against the crashing waves on the beach. "You look like you have something."

As he looked up at the house, his expression of concentration deepened. "The scent of the panther is here, but it's stronger than it was on that stretch of beach. It's almost as if she came to a halt here for some reason and walked around. Maybe sat down and waited." He scanned the flat-raked and clean sand for hints as to why.

"You see anything?" Emma asked, looking down. "I'm not even sure what we're looking for here."

"No, I don't see anything. I'm not sure I expect to. It's far too clean." Renzo frowned. "The wealthy people out here have their staff come out and rake the sand, so it looks presentable. That would remove any evidence."

"They rake sand so it looks presentable?

Presentable to who? Poseidon? They do everything they can to chase people off here," I said with enough disdain to get my point across. "These people put down those PVC pipe-looking markers to keep people off their beach because they don't want visitors, but they send their poorly paid servants out here to rake the sand so it'll look good?" I exhaled and looked up at the house. "I'm sure that makes sense to a rich person."

"Tell us how you really feel, Astra," Emma quipped.

"Sorry. It just seems ridiculous."

Renzo remained silent for another moment before taking a few steps south. "It's more than the panther stopping here." He walked back toward us. "This is as far as the big cat went. If I take a few steps that way, the scent immediately fades."

"Okay, so there are two ways to leave from here," Emma said, looking around. "By water, into the ocean, maybe picked up by a boat. Or into that house. Well, three ways. She could have also gone back the way we came." Her sharp eyes darted here and there. "Yeah, I think that's all."

"Well, unless she went up." I pointed to the blue sky above us.

"Panthers can't fly."

"But remember, this is a divine jaguar of some sort," Renzo remarked, crossing his arms. "We don't really know what its capabilities are or aren't."

Emma cursed under her breath. "So, what do we believe is the most likely scenario in this case? I mean, the simplest thing to do would be to go knock on that door and ask if anyone has seen anything or where their security cameras are pointed." She looked at the get-off-my-beach posts. "Anyone who would poke those things into a white sand beach to keep people away must have security cameras."

"Do we know anything about who lives there?" I asked Renzo. "This is your town; you must know these people."

"That house belongs to Delian Loxias—he goes by Dell. He's a psychiatrist, now retired. Never been married, as far as I know. No children."

"Suspicious," Emma murmured.

Renzo looked at her oddly. "Why? You've never been married or had any children."

"You haven't, and neither has Astra. But, as I previously stated, it is suspicious."

"I don't understand. How are we suspicious?" Renzo asked.

"Dude. Seriously?" Emma asked impatiently. "You don't see how there's anything suspicious about the three of us?" Before Renzo could answer, Emma chuckled. "Okay, werewolf. None of us are suspicious at all."

Renzo awkwardly shifted his gaze away.

"He must've been one heck of a psychiatrist to afford a place like that," I said with a nod. "I know psychiatrists do well these days, but that type of wealth? That seems a little bit beyond what even a doctor would make."

The house wasn't as large as the wine god's—I wondered if anything in Palm Beach was—but it was still enormous. Made of gleaming white stone, it featured black shutters on the windows and massive white columns supporting the roof of a large wraparound porch. The lawn was lush and well-kept, and in the center was a statue of a woman in a long gown. Two massive black Mercedes sedans were parked one in front of the other in the driveway to the side of the home.

"Nice cars," I added. A concrete walkway was laid down from the beach to the house, splitting in two directions. One direction went to the porch and the other to an oversized garage next to the Mercedes in the driveway. "But I do have a question. That's a two-car garage, and two high-end vehicles are parked in the driveway. We're all car people." I looked at Emma and Renzo. "Odd, right?"

For the non-car people: the winds blow salt air and spray off the ocean. The sun and salt air near the coast can be highly damaging to a car's finish. Almost no one of any means (or with a brain in their head) would leave their expensive cars exposed to the elements in their driveway if they had a garage nearby.

"Why would you keep two cars in your driveway instead of in your garage?" Renzo asked quietly, giving a voice to the question in my head. He frowned, but not in a reproachful way. "I don't know, people like that with more money than sense? There could be a reason."

"A reason other than having a panther locked in the garage?" Emma asked.

"And we think we should do what?" I asked, turning to the werewolf. "Knock on the door and ask to speak with the owner?"

"No," he said with a frown. "I believe we should proceed with caution. Everyone on this beachfront appears to be very interested in who is on the beach. So let's just sit here and wait.

Maybe a butler will come out, and we'll be able to get some answers."

* * *

IT WASN'T long before a man appeared on the porch. He turned to face the waves.

Or us.

Okay, he was probably looking at us.

"Dell?" I asked Renzo.

He nodded.

The porch was raised above the ground like a small stage in the middle of a larger one. The physician was motionless, his palms resting on the handrail. Even though he was too far away to see his face, I got the feeling he would come over and say hello—but I was baffled as to why. The man radiated friendliness.

We stood at the property's edge and watched him.

"Do we wave?" Emma asked. "I feel like we should wave."

"He hasn't waved," I pointed out.

Emma cleared her throat. "Look, Renzo. I'm not questioning you or anything, but are you certain that the panther's scent ends right in front of this guy's house? Is it possible that it kept walking down the beach to the south? You're absolutely certain?"

That was a lot of questions for someone not wanting to question.

"Where's this coming from, Emma?" I asked, but she didn't answer.

"I'm reasonably sure, yes," the detective told Emma, sounding defensive.

"So you're *not* sure?" Emma's question sounded like an accusation.

"It's a scent, Emma. I told you what I thought, but am I certain that my guess was correct? No. It's an odor. It could be affected by a hundred multiple variables. There is wind, transference, and small details deteriorate with time. For all I know, the neighbor could have raked the sand with Febreeze." He crossed his arms in front of him in a casual manner, but he looked uncomfortable. "I'm giving you the best information I have."

"Wouldn't that be something different?" she muttered as she turned to face the man on the porch.

Renzo gave her a stern look. "What does that even mean?"

Following that remark, the man gently pushed himself off the porch railing and walked toward the pathway. His movements were slow, fluid, and unhurried, as if he was simply walking to the beach to watch the sunset. Emma and Renzo continued to argue behind me, but I kept my gaze fixed on the man making his way to the beach.

There was something about him…

I couldn't put my finger on it, but something about the way he moved, the way he stood—it was strangely familiar. Like I'd seen it before.

But as he got closer, his features clearer, I knew that couldn't be the case.

I'd never seen him before in my life.

I *knew* it.

But still…

There was an oddity to the way he walked. It didn't seem to have anything to do with his gait. It wasn't his posture. It was something else. Something…

It was hard to pinpoint.

I could see his face as he got closer. His skin was tanned, and he had a flawless complexion. His brows were straight, his nose was straight, and his lips were set in a perpetual, contented smile. Dell was so symmetrical that he could have been a statue created by a master mathematician. The man was a little older, but not by much. He could be forty years old.

Emma was the second to notice his approach.

I was actually surprised that either of them noticed anything at all given how they were bickering about...whatever they were going on about. But she did, in fact, notice when she lucked into rolling her eyes in the same direction as Mr. Loxias.

"Wait a minute, hold the phone. Is that guy coming down here?"

"Emma, we need to talk about this," Renzo cautioned her, but she shook her head.

"No, we need to pay attention to the psychiatrist," she said blithely, but her body was tense. I'd been so preoccupied with Loxias that I'd missed Emma and Renzo's argument, but whatever it had been about? It got under Emma's skin. "That's why we're here, remember?"

"There's something off about that guy," I told the detective and Emma.

Emma looked at him. He was wearing a pair of khaki shorts, a white polo shirt, and very classy, dark brown loafers. "What do you mean?" she asked. "To me, he appears to be a typical preppy rich guy from Palm Beach, always dressed for a yacht party." She looked toward a private dock. "There's the yacht."

The man entered the beach by passing through the gate.

As I watched him close the gap between us, I had an odd thought.

The surroundings appeared almost alien to him. Even with his grace and apparent ease, his shoes made no sound on the sand, and his movements were surprisingly precise. I shook my head to get rid of the strange thought.

"Hello!" he told us with a wave and a smile. "I'm Dell. And you, my friends, are…?"

"Not your friends?" Emma asked, sounding surprised at his friendly welcome. "I don't believe we've ever met before." She looked at the privacy posts stuck in Dell's section of the beach. "And you people don't seem very welcoming to outsiders."

"Of course you're my friends," Dell said warmly, his smile growing wider. "Why would you consider someone you've just met and know nothing about to be your adversary? That appears to be a difficult way to go through life. What's more, that kind of suspicion is toxic."

"I bet you were a barrel of fun in therapy," I commented.

"I wasn't, though I did try to keep people from going too dark too quickly. Therapy is a difficult and complex method of gaining understanding and knowledge," Dell explained, his smile unwavering. "The mind is a perplexing organ, and we only have a limited understanding of its function and purpose."

Nobody cares, dude.

"So you're a psychiatrist, then?" Emma asked.

"I am," he said, nodding. "I'm a lot of things. It's all a matter of perspective, I suppose."

"Did you kidnap your neighbor's panther?" Renzo asked sternly, cutting off any further pleasantries.

I glared at him, worried that his confrontational demeanor had turned off our preppy visitor with the mysterious garage. "Hey, Renzo, anyone ever tell you that you have all the subtlety of a walrus on the attack?"

"I am not a walrus," Renzo answered darkly.

"Goo goo g'joob," Emma finished. She held up her hand. "Sorry. I had to."

"You did not have to," I whispered.

"Hey," Emma said, raising her eyebrow. "I'm on vacation. Lighten up."

Dell didn't seem fazed by Renzo's question or Emma's decision to quote the Beatles in the middle of a seaside interrogation. "Detective Renzo, I would never kidnap anyone. I have nothing to hide, and it would be an honor to show you around my home. You can see for yourself." He stepped back and held out his arm. "My sister is in town for a holiday, but it's just the two of us. And the staff, of course." He smiled widely. "They'd love for someone else to see the holiday decorations."

"I bet," Emma said.

"You bet?" Dell asked. "Do you like to gamble? My dear friend once told me that a bet is a gamble in which the winner believes the loser deserves to lose more than the loser deserves to win." He frowned. "That's not a good attitude. A bet is a cruel thing, in a way." He smiled. "I would never bet on anything. Life is too important."

Emma stared at him and then turned to give me a private look as if to say, "Is this guy serious?" Next to her, Renzo's eyes darted toward Dell's house, then back to us. It was a quick movement, but it telegraphed his discomfort with the doctor's invitation.

"Mr. Loxias," Emma said. "We'd be honored."

I guess Renzo would get over it.

* * *

A FRAME of linked Caduceus symbols was etched into the glass patio door. Following the others into the house, I was greeted by a magical overspread of white Christmas lights twinkling brightly all around. The room, a living area, was dominated by a massive tree in the corner with garlands of lights surrounding it.

I detected a strong peppermint scent in the air as if we'd just missed some ritual in which dozens of candy canes were melted. It permeated everything, and my sinuses cleared up like I'd snorted Vicks.

"What do you think?" Dell asked us, his face expectant.

The inside of the house was as beautiful as the outside, and I said so.

Dell's face beamed again.

Emma leaned over to examine an intricate nativity display.

"Do you follow him?" Loxias asked her excitedly. "The child?"

The child?

Who says that?

Emma narrowed her eyes, looking up. "That's a bit of a controversial topic to bring up with a stranger, isn't it?"

Renzo rubbed his nose.

"Controversial?" Dell asked, his smile brightening. "I didn't think it was, no. In what way?"

Emma was about to answer, but I cut her off. "In the way that if the person you're talking to isn't interested in hearing about your religious bull, it's weird to bring it up."

"Religious bull?"

"Yes."

"Like a taurobolium?" he asked, referencing Roman Empire practices involving sacrificial bulls. "Or the document from the pope?"

I looked at him with astonishment. "Neither. As in foolish religious hokum forced on people to control them."

"You think that's what that is?" Dell asked me, glancing at the nativity.

"Kinda do. Yeah."

"What a cruel world this can be, Astra," Dell said gravely. "I thought the story of the Christ child was a beautiful one. Control is not the thing I took away from the words He spoke." Dell's eyes suddenly shone with sharp intelligence. "Have you ever been a believer, Ms. Arden?" He looked as if he wanted to say more.

"Me?" I asked, suddenly uncomfortable.

Renzo rubbed his nose again, his face pinched

as if he were in pain. The werewolf looked like he was having an allergic reaction to something. His cheeks were—

Wait a minute.

I looked at Dell.

He looked back expectantly.

In my head, I replayed our conversation thus far with Delian Loxias. As I went over it, I realized that I never mentioned my name to him during those conversations. Not once. He'd called Renzo "Detective Renzo" down at the beach, come to think of it. And Renzo never displayed his badge or introduced himself.

Which was probably not a good thing. We should have said who we were before coming into the guy's house. If there was evidence of a crime here, it might be inadmissible. Then again, it's not like Dionysus would be filing a lawsuit or a police report for his magic panther.

"Who are you?" I asked him bluntly.

"I'm Delian," he said quickly. "Dell for short. Mr. Loxias works as well. That's why your friend addressed me by my name."

"No," I said, staring at him. "That's not what I mean. You knew our names before we told you. I'm Astra. That's Renzo and Emma." I pointed. "But somehow, you knew that."

I remained silent, trying to think of what he'd gained by keeping what he knew from us, but nothing came to mind. Though...

He hadn't really hidden anything—in fact, he'd shown his hand down at the beach.

We'd simply missed it.

And then walked into the dude's house.

Like idiots.

"Yes." His smile dimmed for a moment. "I apologize if I frightened you in any way. I've been known to make people feel uneasy with the way I speak at times. I forget that people these days are apprehensive about direct questions and in-depth knowledge."

Rude.

"I don't have a problem with direct questions, but I'm beginning to think you do. So I'm going to ask you again—who are you?"

"Astra," Emma said quietly. "I suppose that's a good question, but not one that anyone can answer easily. I don't think I've ever met anyone that doesn't have a hard time putting themselves into words."

I whirled on her. "Why do you keep defending him? And why did you agree to come up here without knowing much about him?"

She blinked. "Um." She looked at me, frowning. "I don't know."

Renzo moved closer to Emma, shooting Dell a red-eyed glare.

I turned back to the doctor. "Who are you?" I was seriously losing my patience, and I hoped against hope that blindly following this guy didn't just put us all in terrible danger.

"Well, Astra, who do I think I am?" Dell asked me. "I'm a good person. I'm an honest person. I'm a person who wants the best for the world around me." He cocked his head to the side. "And who are you?"

"Buddy, I am seriously starting to lose my patience with you," I snapped. "This isn't about me."

"Isn't it?"

I didn't know how to respond. Something about his question had struck me speechless.

"Let's get out of here," Renzo said suddenly. "It's not the neighbor we're looking for." He turned and walked toward the door.

Emma blinked. "Renzo?" She seemed to see him for the first time, eyes red and nose swollen. "Jeez, Eddie, what happened to you? Are you okay?"

"It's no big deal." He tapped his nose. "I'm allergic to peppermint."

It was an easy answer, but I was pretty sure he wasn't allergic to peppermint.

I read somewhere that peppermint was toxic to dogs, and there was something about it they straight up didn't like. So it wouldn't surprise me if wolves had the same issue.

I narrowed my eyes.

Had Dell done that on purpose? Doused his house in peppermint oil to confuse any tracking dogs looking for a stolen panther?

Or did he know what Renzo was?

"Who are you?" I asked, my tone confrontational. "Enough with the cryptic song and dance and the jolly Christmas cheer. How do you know who we are?"

"I always do," he said simply. "All the time, every time."

Who the heck was this weirdo? "That's not an answer."

"Can you think of a better way to welcome you to my home?" He gestured toward the twinkling tree. "I didn't do anything threatening, Astra. If you think I'm a danger to you, you're welcome to leave. I won't stop you, but I want you to see what I have to show you first." His eyes flashed with sudden intensity, focused entirely on me. "I know who I think you are."

"What do you mean?" I asked.

"He's messing with you," Renzo said, his voice harsh. "Let's go."

"I am not messing with anyone," Dell said directly to me, answering Renzo's statement without acknowledging him. "I want to show you something. It's the reason I asked you to come here."

I folded my arms. "Well, if you know so much about me, you should know that I don't like being played."

"I'm not playing you," he said, his voice soft and warm and filled with understanding and kindness. It was like a drug. "I know where you come from and what you do." His eyes narrowed. "I know what happened to you in the past. I know why you're here in Palm Beach." His voice grew louder, more insistent. "And I know what you need to do right now, what you need to see right now, to heal."

Wait a minute...

The Caduceus symbol on the door...

The peppermint oil...

The strange movements, strange pull...

The card Ami texted about...

We stood facing each other like two strangers searching for something missing, but I couldn't say anything. He waited patiently for me to speak. Eventually, all I could manage was, "Oh, you have to be kidding me."

He grinned as if my saying little pleased him. As if he sensed I knew who he was. "Yes, Astra—I am Apollo," the man said with a wide smile. "And I rarely kid."

CHAPTER NINE

*A*pollo.

The god of…what was he the god of? The sun? Wolves? Doctors. I think. I pulled out my phone and texted Ami, letting her know that the card she mentioned might have another meaning—then I glanced up at the werewolf. Was he even in any danger? The card that glowed wasn't the star card. Since it wasn't the star card, it could mean anything, really. Especially if we were dealing with gods.

I AM SITTING IN APOLLO'S LIVING ROOM, I texted.

APOLLO WHO? Ami texted back.

APOLLO APOLLO. HE LIVES A FEW

MANSIONS DOWN FROM DIONYSUS. The gold-tufted walls exuded a sense of grandeur, complemented by gold-finished table lamps and chandeliers I wasn't sure weren't made of actual gold. Sofas, armchairs, and built-in benches provided ample seating capacity.

ARE YOU KIDDING? APOLLO APOLLO?

THAT'S THE ONE. Various sun mirrors decorated the walls, and an extensive sound system played an instrumental that sounded distinctly Greek. IS PALM BEACH THE NEW OLYMPUS? I asked her.

NO. Ami texted back almost immediately. Then, a few seconds later, she added: IDK. GETTING MOM.

Yep.

Probably a good idea.

The ocean's foamy waves could be seen through the large, floor-to-ceiling windows. Archie swooped in to perch on one of the wingback chairs, and I winced as his talons dug in. "Nice digs," he said and then preened his feathers.

I approached the chair, sat, and leaned in. "Is that all you have to say?"

The owl's head whipped up and thrust forward toward me. "What do you want me to say?" His eyes gazed over the room. "Something you need explained? Because if there is, you're not as bright as I thought you were."

"Archie, my friend," Apollo's rich baritone rang out from across the room, greeting the owl warmly. "It is good to see you! You're looking well for a philosophical metaphor!" The god laughed. "Is your latest assignment going well?"

I suppose that would be me.

Archie narrowed his eyes. "We're here, aren't we?" Apollo didn't respond. "You have any rabbits?" Archie asked the god gruffly.

Archie accepted Apollo's existence—and location—with such a casual symbolic shrug of his little bird shoulders that my suspicious hackles shot up toward the gold-leaf ceiling. Did the owl know what we would find here? Why didn't he speak up? Did he know these gods—Dionysus, Ariadne, and Apollo—lived in Florida? That they were in Palm Beach? Why not warn me about what we might be getting ourselves into?

"What do you mean, we're here?" I asked. "Did you know we would meet Apollo?" The bird blinked but didn't respond. "No answer?" Another blink. "And if you did, why didn't you tell me? Aren't you supposed to be on my side?"

Archie eyed me with obvious irritation. "You

are more disappointing than an unsalted pretzel sometimes." Then, he turned away from me and continued preening his feathers as if his appearance was the most critical thing in the world.

Something was going on here.

Something.

But what?

I stood up and faced Apollo. "Look, did you take Dionysus's panther?"

Apollo shook his head silently. "Of course not. After Hermes stole my fifty cows that time?" He shuddered. "What a nightmare that turned out to be, all the lying and lyre trading and...ugh." Then he brightened. "I did get the gift of prophecy out of it, so there's that." Apollo smiled. "Anyway, I didn't take the panther."

"You say that like it's supposed to be obvious, but it's not obvious. In fact, it's the opposite of obvious," I told him, crossing my arms. "If even half of the stories about you people are true...I mean, you constantly fight among yourselves, are completely irrational, often unfair, and you get so jealous of one another I'm surprised three of you are still alive thousands of years later to be neighbors. Why wouldn't I—"

"You must be mistaken, Astra. No gods were ever killed in our myths," Apollo told me.

"They're immortal with a capital I. I-M-M-O-R-T-A-L," Archie spelled out with exasperation. "Do you need a dictionary, or are you familiar with the word?" When I didn't answer, Archie looked at Apollo. "You got a dictionary?"

"I don't need a dictionary," I snapped at the bird, glancing to my right. I stopped as my gaze was drawn to a photograph hanging on the wall behind Archie. The image depicted Apollo and Alexarchos, the Dionysiac priest, enjoying themselves at a party. They stood close together, each holding a flute of champagne.

"Astra, what's wrong?" Emma asked.

"I'm starting to feel like I'm being played," I told her, searching through the faces in the other photographs for any I recognized. Dionysus. His wife.

My mother.

None jumped out at me.

Emma's brow furrowed as she watched me. "Okay. What do you mean, played? In what way?"

"I don't know." I stalked across the room (as if angry) and directed a meaningful glare at the pictures on the shelf. "I feel like the other paranormals in the situation are keeping things from me." I placed one hand on my hip and directed my other toward the photographs (pointing my finger clandestinely). "Like there's a bunch of information people aren't telling us."

Emma gave a subtle nod.

"Well, there's always information people aren't telling you, Astra," Apollo said as my friend moved across the room toward the photos. "Sometimes they're trying to hide what they've done, of course, but sometimes they are not telling you because you're simply not ready to hear the information." The god held out his hands toward me. "Are you ready to hear—and see—the information?"

"What are you talking about?" While Emma leaned in and examined photographs and various trinkets adorning the shelves, the god and I engaged in a back and forth. "We literally walked into this house to ask you about the panther. Obviously, I'm ready to hear the information."

"I'm not talking about the panther."

"Then what are you talking about?"

"Grab my hands, let me take you on a journey of the present," he said excitedly. "Read me, Astra. You took Ari's hands and allowed her to show you the past. If you read me, Astra, you will have a much different experience. I am concerned not with the past or the paths that you took to get here. I'm all about the now."

* * *

"THIS WHOLE THING is starting to remind me of something, but I can't think of it," I told Emma as we stood outside on the porch. There was something familiar about this whole thing. Maybe not the stolen panther, but the paranormal delve into the past and then the present. "Something else is going on here, though."

"It's 'A Christmas Carol,'" Eddie said. We both looked at him with puzzled expressions. "Oh, come on. Didn't either of you ever read that book? Or see the movie?" He looked back and forth between us. "Ebenezer Scrooge? Tiny Tim?" Eddie's arms bulged through his shirt, and a furrow across his brow indicated a frown.

"The guy that plays the ukulele?" Emma asked, frowning.

Eddie chuckled. "You two really are completely out of touch, aren't you? It's one of the most famous holiday tales ever told. Do you two do anything but work?" He shook his head in amusement. "I don't even know why I asked that. This is your vacation, right? Both of you?"

"I'm not completely out of touch," I muttered, giving the werewolf a dark glare. "I just didn't read a lot of human books when I was growing up. We sure didn't say anything about Christmas when I lived in Imperatorial City."

"I've kind of vaguely heard of it, but I'm not familiar with it," Emma said. "Anyway, are you saying we are in a book or something?" She cocked her head. "That would be new."

"No, I don't think we're in a book," Eddie said. "But I feel like some of the things happening seem to parallel 'A Christmas Carol.' Here, look. The story is straightforward. A business owner that isn't a very nice guy is visited by three ghosts at Christmas. A ghost of Christmases past, the ghost of Christmas present, and the ghost of Christmas future."

"I can't see ghosts, so that's not what's going on." I shrugged. "Or, if it is, I wouldn't know it. Because I can't see them."

"You're taking what I'm saying too literally. I'm not saying ghosts are running around exactly like they were in the book. It's—look, I've been listening to what these gods have been saying.

They are mostly focused on you, Astra—not Emma and me."

I shrugged again. "That's because I'm a witch, and this has to do with the coven. There's nothing odd about that. I may be the least of coven members, but I am still a coven member."

"No, I don't think that's it."

I looked at Emma. "You don't?"

"If you think about it, it doesn't have to do with the coven, not really," Emma pointed out as she watched the seagulls scamper around on the beach. "Dionysus accused Athena of stealing the panther. That's how your family became involved. This situation didn't involve Apollo at all as far as I can tell—and yet we were led right to this house by the panther's scent."

"Where the sun god is asking you to go on a psychic trip about the present." Eddie leaned against a column. He was framed against the waves, the sky a brilliant hue of blue that shined out from the horizon. "You commented back at the other house that you'd seen an incredible amount of the past when you grabbed Ari's hands —something, by the way, she was pretty insistent on."

"Yeah, but it wasn't *my* past. It was *her* past." I looked into the house and studied the expression on Apollo's face. Could this all be some gigantic ruse? "You think this is some kind of elaborate mystery play just for me?"

"What's a mystery play?" Emma asked.

"They were medieval plays that focused on representations of Bible stories and churches. It was a way to get religious lessons across to people engagingly and entertainingly," Eddie said. Then, turning to me, he nodded. "Your coven does a version of them sometimes when you do rituals that act out the myths, right?"

Before I could answer, Emma jumped in. "Astra, if these guys are real," she said, glancing back toward the large house, "Athena is, too. If she has the power to set up the whole star card thing, she probably has the power to set up this soap opera-type sideshow here. I mean, if that's what it is."

"Which we don't know for sure," Eddie added.

"Alexarchos was totally freaked out this morning. He was panicking, practically hyperventilating. I don't know that he could pretend that level of fear—and Dionysus doesn't seem disciplined enough to pull off an elaborate hoax like this."

Eddie lowered his voice, his eyes on mine. "I hate to make an obvious point, but these are gods we're talking about. Do we really know what they're capable of faking and what they are not?"

"When you did your magic hands reading of the stable, you didn't see anything that would help us," Emma added. "Don't you think you should have?"

I frowned. "If someone paranormal took the panther, though, that's easily explainable." My half-clenched fist tapped my thigh, and then I exhaled harshly. "I see what you're saying, though."

"I have to tell you, I think you're right—both of you. Something else is going on here, and I think it has to do with you, Astra." Emma and I locked gazes. "You know, you've been really fighting the idea that Athena gave you the power that you have. Even when you say things that sort of accept it, you sound like you're dismissing it."

"So?"

"So maybe Athena has lost patience." Emma pointed in the house. "You know, your familiar owl hasn't come out here to talk to us in our little confab. Not once."

"You can't really read into that. Apollo is giving him rabbit jerky."

Eddie looked at both of us. "I still see too many parallels to 'A Christmas Carol.' Granted, they're small, but we should examine the possibility. The gods like stories. And that one"—he glanced toward the house—"really seems to be into Christmas."

"Are Apollo and Athena particularly close?" Emma asked.

I shrugged. "I don't know."

"Look, the Dickens story is about the possibility of redemption," Detective Renzo told me, his voice serious. "I don't know what you've done in your past and what you haven't, so I couldn't speak to any of that. But it's also about the damaging effects of isolation—Scrooge doesn't feel like he needs anyone. He's isolated. Dismissive. The ghosts come to him, and he scoffs at them in the beginning. He doesn't believe any of what is being shown."

"Sounds familiar," Emma pointed out.

I glared at her. "And what is he shown?" I asked Renzo.

"Things that try to persuade him that family is important, that his actions have consequences, and that his actions are a result of his beliefs—and his beliefs need to change," he responded.

"Okay, say you're right. Say this is my very own *Greek Yule Carol*." I glared at Archie through the open door, slightly irritated that the owl was avoiding any explanation for what was going on. He stopped eating the rabbit jerky as if sensing my stare and turned. "What can I expect? What do I have to do?"

Eddie shifted uncomfortably against the column. "In one word? Change."

* * *

"So is it?" I asked the sun god after we finished our discussion on the porch. "Is that what's going on? Did you all create this big mystery on my vacation as some kind of elaborate divine ruse to teach me a lesson?"

"It *is* an absolutely wonderful story, isn't it?" Apollo responded with excitement—without, by the way, answering the direct questions I put to him. "The three ghosts coming to change one person. Realizing that one person and how they value their fellow man is so important. It is so meaningful and matters to so many people! Even one person being greedy or mean or a miser can be so damaging to so many."

"I never saw the movie or read the book," I told the god dryly. "Again, is that what you all are doing? Did you fake the panther kidnapping just to get me here?"

Archie made a frustrated noise and scowled at me.

"I didn't fake anything, dear Astra," Apollo replied, stunned. "You must be confusing me with Hermes. I'd never meet someone under false pretenses." He smirked. "However, Dr. Goldberg stated that the ability to lie is a human achievement. It's one of those extraordinary abilities that set them apart from all other species."

"You're not human," I pointed out. "Neither is Hermes."

"He really doesn't like Hermes, does he?" Emma asked Eddie.

"I don't think I'm going to speak for god here," Eddie countered in a noncommittal tone. "They can be a little sensitive."

"Hermes gave me many things. Well, traded me—with Hermes, there's always some type of price. I don't hate him. I don't even dislike him," Apollo told the two. "As for the lies we were talking about, there are many types of lies," the god added, his expression sincere. "Which ones, in particular, are you concerned with?"

I looked at Archie. "Do you really have nothing to say about any of this?"

"What do you want me to say?" he asked lazily

and plucked another rabbit jerky strip from the plate. "Half the time when I talk, you don't bother to listen to me, anyway."

"A divine gift like that, and you scoff?" Apollo shook his head sadly.

My cheeks pinked hotly. "That's not true. I do not *scoff*."

"See, that would be a 'guilty secret' lie," Apollo observed. "It stems from the fear of being shamed. The lie's purpose is to prevent other people from finding out about things you feel would meet with disapproval." The sun god looked proud of himself. "Your guilty secret is that you don't listen to the owl at least half the time—or enough that you felt the need to deny his accusation."

"Maybe I denied it because it's not tr—you know what? Forget it. Stay out of this!" I told him.

Apollo smiled. "Oh, no need to get defensive, Astra. It's perfectly normal. Everyone does it."

"Why won't you just answer my question?"

"What question?"

"Did you all create this big mystery on my vacation to teach me a lesson?"

Apollo stepped forward, his eyes flickering with a golden light that seemed to shine from deep within him. He extended his hands. "All of your answers, Astra, are within your grasp."

I hesitated.

Then I ripped off my gloves and took a step forward.

CHAPTER TEN

"I love you, Daraja."

I heard the woman's voice before I saw anything. There was a darkness, a haze, around the outline of…something. It was in front of me, or I was in front of it. I couldn't tell. The fog swirling around me made it difficult to get my bearings. "What is this?" I murmured, and my voice sounded like it was wrapped in cotton. "What is happening? Where am I?"

"Where you were," Apollo responded. "You're still in Palm Beach, of course. But you're also somewhere else. *We* are also somewhere else, to be more accurate."

"I don't understand."

Apollo paused for a moment and then said kindly, "You will."

Suddenly, I could see her through the darkness. She was there but...not there. Faced away from me, I couldn't identify her. She leaned over a dark-skinned girl wrapped in a pink comforter cuddled up on a bed. "I love you, too," the little girl said enthusiastically to the woman, her voice high pitched and her response lightly accented. "I love you, especially when we get ice cream." The child beamed with a big grin.

What was this?

I could feel Apollo's hands in mine, but it didn't feel like we were standing across from each other. Instead, we seemed to stand side by side, the god holding my right hand. I cocked my head to look at him. "What are you showing me?"

"Things you might need to see, of course. Now a question for you. Do you think she looks happy?" he asked, his voice echoed as if we were in an empty room.

"Yes, but who is she?" I asked. "What is this?"

"You don't remember?"

The woman leaned in again and kissed the girl.

"Should I remember?"

I gasped as she pushed herself off the bed and

turned to face me. "I know her. That's Marianna
Black, the woman who was abducted when I first
returned to Forkbridge."

"Your first star card case, yes." Apollo looked
pleased. "And that, in the bed, is the little girl
from the Nigerian orphanage," he told me. "After
you rescued Marianna, she returned to Nigeria
and adopted the little girl. The experience she
went through made her realize she didn't want to
wait for the perfect man to become a mother."

Marianna smiled as she walked out of the
hazy frame, and the lights in the girl's room
flickered off. We stood there, silently watching
the little girl roll around in the brightly decorated
twin bed.

"The scene you're looking at? It could never
have happened without you. Without Athena's
gift and your use of it."

Daraja reached out and grabbed a doll,
murmuring, "We're so lucky, Raggedy. Mommy
said we could get ice cream tomorrow. But we
have to be quiet and go to sleep, so shhhh."

The frame shifted as if a camera was leaving a
scene. Now the break in the dense smoke moved
down a long corridor and into a small nook off a
large, airy kitchen. Mariana sat across from a
pleasant-looking gentleman sipping a mug of

something hot. "He's nice to her," Apollo told me. "Reliable and considerate. They're not getting married or anything, at least not yet. But he's good to the little girl, and he's good to her, and he's willing to wait until she's comfortable with a deeper commitment."

I was happy for her.

Relieved.

Better than that jerk ex of hers.

The image flickered and changed as the memory passed through my mind. Suddenly, I felt dizzy, as if we were flying through the air. I held Apollo's hand tighter.

"I told you. I'm not sure how she feels about me, Mother," Jason Bishop said as he and his mother sat at an outdoor table together. The table was square, thickly lacquered, and supported by square legs. The restaurant was unfamiliar. "Besides, the ghost she saw on Halloween rattled her. I'm sure it did." He leaned in, his lips pursed into a tight smile. "Or maybe it was me who shook her up."

"You are aware Guru Bernie rescinded those ridiculous rules because he was certain the two of you were dating," Mayor Thornton explained to her son. "Well, not *sure* you were dating, and it wasn't the only reason, of course," she added, sipping a glass of wine. "But he was grateful for the Ardens' assistance with everything and felt it was time for those rules to be retired. For our two communities to ally with one another." Mayor Thornton narrowed her eyes. "But he did expect the two of you—"

"Mother, can't you just let it drop for one dinner?" Jason cut her off, looking pained. The night was clear, the air calm, but his expression was neither.

"I can. Of course, I can."

"Thank you."

After a few moments of silence, Jason's mother inquired, "Do you think she's worried you're seeing other girls? Is that the problem?"

"Mother!"

His mother's face was expressionless as she looked at him. "What? It's just a question, Jason. Why are you so defensive?"

I should have realized he was talking about me from the beginning of the scene. I knew he wanted to ask me out for a date, and I knew I'd been avoiding the question. Also, his mother's interest in the two of us having a relationship was news.

"Okay, interesting development. Mayor

Thornton likes me. Awesome. We should go," I told Apollo.

We didn't.

"I'm not sure she believes in anything, Mom."

"What are you talking about, Jason?"

He fingered the stem of the wine glass in front of him. "Since the Halloween festival, she hasn't said much. We used to talk when we went running in the morning, you know? We stop at the park and have long conversations about so many things."

"You still go running, the two of you, don't you?"

"We do." Jason shrugged. "To be honest, I don't think I was as helpful as I could have been with what happened in Cassandra," he muttered as he grabbed his knife and fork to cut into a steak on his plate. "In the end, I needed rescuing," he said after a brief pause. "It was humiliating. Maybe it's me who isn't as open anymore. I mean, how do you ask a woman out after that? She's said nothing about any of it. Not how she feels about what happened. Nothing."

What was there to talk about? We did what we had to do.

"That's not necessarily a drawback, you know," his mother responded. Jason looked surprised. "Oh, not the rescue thing." Mayor Thornton waved her hand in the air. "That she hasn't said anything. A woman who doesn't tell too much of her feelings usually has very deep feelings."

"Or none at all."

The mayor made a noise like a football going flat.

"Mother, I'm not good with women." Jason shook his head. "I don't know how to..." He frowned, tossing down his utensils with a clank. "Why am I talking about this with you? I don't know what I'm doing."

Mayor Thornton's face softened with sympathy as she gazed across the table at her son. "Jason, don't be silly. You do know. You just fear failure." She pointed her finger. "You also seem to be struggling with the idea of a woman that's not a wilting flower. Of course she doesn't need you to protect her, Jason. But that shouldn't be the basis of a relationship, anyway."

"I don't think that's what I'm doing. That's not what I think." Jason's face sagged, and light seemed to retreat from his eyes. "Okay, maybe it is. I don't know. The only thing I seem to know for sure is that it's terrifying to have such a strong desire for something."

My jaw dropped.

It was difficult to listen to him sound so full of hope and deep desire. It was so private, so raw—so wrong to be listening. My face burned with embarrassment. "Okay, I'm not kidding. This is wrong," I whispered to Apollo even though I was almost sure no one could hear us. "We should go. We shouldn't be listening to this."

The god said nothing, and we still went nowhere.

"I understand you're afraid of being hurt," his mother said, finishing the last bit of the pear on her plate. "There are risks, of course. But, my son, there are risks in anything in life."

"Mother, I feel like I am falling—"

* * *

MY EYES WIDENED as I yanked my hands away from Apollo's. I felt woozy—as if I'd been swept away by a strong tide. I shook my head and tried to concentrate. "That was wrong," I told the god. "That was as a private conversation as private conversations get. I can't believe you brought me there to listen to that."

"Astra, are you okay?" Emma asked from somewhere behind me.

I kept my eyes glued to the calm and unapologetic god. Apollo's expression was hard to read, but when he spoke, his voice seemed kind. How did this self-involved jerk manage to sound kind and considerate all the time?

"Why not? Why can you not believe I brought you to listen?" he asked serenely.

"It was private!" I stared at him, trying to understand why he'd shown me what he did. "You completely violated Jason's privacy. If he wanted me to know what he said, he would tell me." I turned my eyes away, feeling ashamed and angry and confused and a dozen other things all at once. "What are you trying to prove? What is the point of all this?" I shook my head mechanically back and forth, attempting to clear it.

"I'm not trying to prove anything," Apollo said. "I have no specific agenda. I'm just showing you the truth."

"Whatever truth that contained, it was private."

"What are the two of you talking about?" Emma asked again, more insistent.

"He just took me to overhear a conversation between Jason and his mother. A very personal conversation that Apollo the nosy god seems to believe we had a right to overhear, even though it was private."

"It was a truth any ghost passing by the two of them would be able to hear. Remember, my dear, the concept of privacy in Cassandra is very different than it is anywhere else. They have a much different concept of privacy," Apollo tilted his head, "and he had no expectation of privacy there."

"He certainly expected I wouldn't be listening."

"I don't know that I would agree. You're a witch. You could if you wanted to. He likely knows that."

"Is one of your superpowers justification? Because I feel like you can justify anything even if it's wrong." I opened my mouth to object but let out a low sigh instead. "Forget it. Fine. Whatever."

"Unsalted pretzel," Archie muttered, watching.

"You wanna get in on this, birdbrain?" I snapped. "You have a viewpoint?"

"Hey, I'm being put through all this, too, you know!" Archie snapped back. "Sucks to find out that you've been making mistakes, doesn't it, toots?"

"What mistakes?" I shot back. "What mistakes have I made?"

"I was talking about me, you self-absorbed twit!" the owl shouted, the words exploding out of him with a flap of his wings. "You worry about your lessons; I'll worry about mine!"

Emma shifted her gaze back and forth between us, her face perplexed. "I don't get it. What happened?" Emma inquired once more.

"That blindingly bright buffoon over there took me to peek in on some people. Mariana Black first," I told her, taken aback by how calm and reasonable my voice sounded. "She adopted that little kid we read about in the paper, by the way. The one in the orphanage. They look happy."

"Wonderful!" My friend smiled. Her smile faded as she examined my expression. "But, I presume, that's not all? And?"

"And he took me to peek in on Jason's dinner with his mother. Talking about some woman he—"

Archie and Apollo burst out laughing at the same time, cutting me off.

"Some woman?" the god asked. "You think the man was talking about some woman?"

"Well, he never said a name, did he? Since Jason never identified who he was talking about, I can't assume—"

"If you're not seeing what he's talking about—or who he's talking about—it's because you don't want to. I'm merely displaying the truth to you, Astra," Apollo said slowly and precisely. "I recognize that reality is more complex than your limited experience prepared you for—"

"Hold up. My limited experience?" The nerve of this guy. "My limited experience says truth is not always about exposing things." I opened my mouth to say something, then quickly shut it again. "It wasn't right. Period."

"Was that all you took from what I showed you?" Apollo waited patiently, his expression expectant in the silent room as everyone watched me struggle.

I took a deep breath and tried once more. "Look, I know this might be anathema to you, but sometimes the truth is that our lives are private. Sometimes people aren't ready to have their secrets exposed. And yes, that is what I took from what you showed me." I'm curious what he saw on my face, because something flashed across his own in response. "That wasn't fair to him. Or to me."

Apollo smiled and nodded to himself. "You are taking this very personally for someone who's refusing to admit the conversation she overheard was about her," he told me.

I wondered at that point what the penalty was for punching a sun god.

Emma turned to Apollo. "Can I ask you a question?"

He nodded once.

"Is there really a missing panther? Or is this all an excuse for you guys to lecture Astra?" Emma waited for Apollo to answer, but again, he remained silent. "The reason I'm asking is that I may be off the clock, and Astra may be off the clock, but Eddie isn't." Emma gestured to her friend. "He might have something more important to do. Like, you know, solve a crime."

"I don't have anything else to do," Eddie said quickly, smiling. "I'm good."

"Okay, great," Emma conceded. "But I still don't have an answer to my question."

"Which is?" Apollo asked.

"Is there a missing panther?"

The god raised an eyebrow and shrugged. "You tell me."

Emma's eyes narrowed in apparent disbelief. "Seriously?"

"You're all going to catch on at some point,"

Apollo said, giving me a frank look. "And it's going to be a good day for us all when you do."

* * *

"IT IS A RIDDLE, wrapped in a mystery, inside an enigma; but perhaps there is a key," Emma said. The three of us were halfway down toward the beach sitting together in one of the many patio necks in Apollo's sloping backyard. Archie remained in the house with the sun god, but I could feel his distant annoyance.

"What key?" I asked her.

"Well, when Winston Churchill said it, it was Russian national interest." I made a face. "The quote. That's who coined the phrase. Winston Churchill. He was talking about Russia."

Helpful.

Okay, not really.

I knew Jason Bishop wanted to ask me out, but I didn't realize his feelings for me were as intense as I'd seen in Apollo's Christmas present vision. Part of me felt guilty for my deliberate avoidance of the topic, the multitude of ways I'd manipulated distance between us to avoid any discussion of anything too personal.

That must have hurt, and it must've felt like rejection.

That was never my intent.

On the other hand, I'd never considered having any relationship with anyone. The military made it nearly impossible—I'd be gone for extended periods, never knowing how long I'd be back in Impy. I only met (a) people doing the same thing with the same stability and time issues or (b) criminals I was arresting.

Well, *accused* criminals.

Innocent or not, they weren't dating material.

"Do you want to talk about what you saw?" Emma asked quietly.

I glanced at her and then at Eddie.

"I can take a walk on the beach for a few minutes if you like," Renzo offered with an easy smile. "I know Emma quite well, but I realize you and I hardly know one another at all. So maybe you'll be more comfortable if I wasn't here."

"You're fine." I shifted on the chair and put my chin in my hand. "To tell you the truth, I feel a little lost right now. I don't know what the heck I'm supposed to do." I looked at Eddie. "Am I supposed to protect you because the Apollo card with the wolf means you're in trouble? Am I on some Yuletide journey of self-discovery? Is there even a case? Is there a reason the two of you are here?" I threw my hands up in the air. "Is Alexarchos even a priest?"

"No," Emma said quickly, sitting up.

"No, what?" I asked.

"You asked if Alexarchos was even a priest." She looked at me, her eyes wide. "No. He's not a priest. Or...well, he couldn't have been when he was in that photo with Apollo, at least."

I thought back to the image of the tattooed goth standing next to the tanned son god. Then it hit me. "The champagne."

She nodded. "The champagne. He was holding alcohol. That means one of two things. He knew Apollo first and then became a Dionysian priest after they met—"

"Or he's lying about being a priest," Eddie finished.

"And there *is* a star card case. Well, more to the point, there's some star card something or another going on here," Emma said, nodding. "I understood everything Archie said in there, and I have ever since we arrived in Palm Beach. I can only understand him when he talks if there's a case going on."

I leaned back in the chair and gazed up at the

clear blue sky. "Okay. Considering the weirdness of all this, I'm sure what *that* means."

I pulled out my phone and looked at the messages. Ami hadn't texted me back since she told me she would get Mom. I frowned. I texted TALKED 2 MOM YET? and put the phone face up on the table to wait for the response.

YEP

I frowned. AND?

GOOD LUCK

My frown deepened. WHAT DOES THAT MEAN?

GOOD LUCK

"Well, that's just great," I muttered and tossed my phone down on the patio table. "Whatever's going on, my sisters and my mother know about it—and they're not gonna share any information." I drummed my fingers on the table. "So did my mother have a hand in it? Or does she just know about it?" I glanced back at the house, my mind racing through the possibilities. "Now, normally, I'd accuse her of all this, but if Alexarchos is still there, he may have just told her what was going on once we left." I slumped in my chair.

"But they're not telling us?" Eddie asked.

"No." Discouraged, I got up and paced the patio

overlook. "But here's the thing," I said as I paced, "Alexarchos told us a story that would accomplish a few things. One, it would pique Emma's interest because it involved crime. Two, it would cause her to reach out to you, Eddie, because it tied in to a case you were working on. I mean, *we* didn't know all this," I said as I turned to face them. "But that doesn't mean someone else didn't."

"You think Eddie's here for a reason?"

"And you," I told Emma. "Think about it. We never would have found Apollo's house if we didn't have a werewolf with us. You and I have no way to follow that scent."

Emma turned to Eddie and repeated, word for word, what I said.

"You know, I can hear her just fine," the Palm Beach detective told Emma.

"Yeah, no, I know. I just like to talk things through myself. It helps me process them." Then she added, "So it's not just about you, it's about all of us?"

I paced more. "I don't know. Maybe."

"To what end, though?" Eddie asked.

I stopped pacing again. "That's the question, isn't it?"

*a*pollo's house was a couple of hundred yards from the beach, the backyard a sloping mess of seating areas. The hike back up wasn't insignificant, and the seating areas seemed oddly placed—far from the house and far from the beach.

As we stepped onto the large terrace, Emma said quietly, "Hey, Astra, there's someone in there talking to Apollo. Did you see anyone come in?"

"No, but I wasn't really paying attention."

"They're right here!" Apollo called out when he noticed us peering in. "Come on in, come on in! My brother heard you were in town and wanted to meet you!" He motioned to the side of the room, where a man was sitting at a chessboard. Archie sat across from him, looking dissatisfied.

Apollo's mysterious brother, short and stocky, with white-blonde hair and a build that suggested he'd been a bodybuilder in his youth, stared at the chess pieces on the board. He wore a wide-brimmed hat with the brim pulled down, lending him a mysterious air. "It's a tricky game, Apollo. I concur."

"It's not complicated; it's very, very simple," Archie exclaimed emphatically. The owl swung his talon at the Queen, knocking her down. "See? It's not so difficult to bring down the Queen, is it?" On the small table, the chess piece rolled around. "You complicate things too much."

"But you've broken the rules," the man said, his tone as gentle as his brother's. "I've been known to break a rule or two in my time, but always with purpose and meaning." The man leaned forward. "What did you just accomplish, Archimedes? What did you achieve by breaking that rule?" The man smiled as he leaned back. "You've been disqualified. I won."

"Why don't you all just climb back up your mountain and stay there?" Archie asked grumpily of the man—though it didn't appear to be a request. It sounded more like a command. "You don't even understand the world any longer, and we live in it, you know. You don't." Archie leaped onto the table and marched across the chessboard, knocking pieces down as he went. "If you were really as powerful as you pretend to be, you'd be more than a style of architecture!"

Archie had a betrayed expression on his face as he looked at the man.

The man returned his gaze calmly, unperturbed by the owl's verbal attack.

"Who is that guy, and why is Archie so angry at him?" I asked Apollo.

"That is my brother, Hermes," Apollo said. His voice was loud enough to be heard throughout the room. "The messenger of the Olympian gods. He is also, of course, a trickster. A psychopomp. The protector of the heralds, travelers, and thieves—"

"I thought tricksters were funny," Emma said. She turned and looked at the serious man. "You don't seem very funny."

"I find myself quite amusing," Hermes responded with a smile.

"You know, whenever I heard all the things you were a god of, I always wondered exactly how that happened," Emma said, pivoting on her heels to get a better look at him. "Those are three pretty divergent groups of people to protect. How do you pick them? Do you pick them, or were you assigned to those people by Zeus?"

"You forgot a few things," he said, pushing out of his chair. "I'm also a shepherd god and a god of boundaries. Gyms. Fighting. Truthfully, I forget half of them until a problem comes up with one of the groups, so I take no offense to your forgetting them." Hermes rose to his feet and turned around, looking at each of us. "It's good to meet all of you."

I moved over to the chessboard. "Why were you giving my owl grief?"

He gave me a half-shrug. "Because it's not your owl and because Archimedes has been struggling with the challenges of boundaries. He's been loaned to you for a purpose, gifted to you for some time for a purpose." Hermes raised an eyebrow at Archie. "That purpose is not to become an insult comic."

"Ouch," the werewolf said, watching.

Again, we're being distracted by things *not a panther*. Things that have nothing to do with a panther. The panther is our goal. The panther is what we're trying to find. We need to stay focused on the panther.

Not that you'd know it from this conversation.

"At this point, should we even bother looking for this panther?" I asked Hermes with exasperation. "You showing up here to chastise the owl for how he's doing in his unpaid job seems pretty planned, if you don't mind me saying so. I'm beginning to wonder if the concept of a stolen panther is just something made up to entice us to chase our tails and wander into your mystery play."

"I don't mind if you say whatever you want, Astra." Hermes grinned. "I'm the gods' messenger and herald. I'm interested in communication. Is it possible to talk things out? Always!" The god reached into his pocket and handed Archie rabbit jerky.

The owl kept his beak in the air, his eyes deliberately looking past the god of communication in an apparent snub—which lasted about five seconds before he gulped down the strip. "You're so easily swayed," I told Archie.

"Am not," he responded, his beak full.

"You should do it more with those who are close to you," Hermes said to me.

"What?"

"Talk."

I gave him an odd look. "I talk to my friends and family all the time."

"Well, you haven't talked to me in a while," a voice in the hallway said. It was a deep voice but married with the echo of a whisper. Like it was coming from somewhere else.

"What was that?" Hermes and Apollo smiled at one another, each sporting a Cheshire cat grin. "Who's here?"

It seemed like there was a shadow of a man standing at the entrance to the hallway. He leaned against the wall, just out of the light. He had his hands in the pockets of his overcoat and his head lowered. He was looking at the floor.

"Eddie, do you see that?" Emma whispered.

"I do," he answered, sounding stunned.

As the outline solidified, I gasped.

It looked up.

"You're dead," I whispered.

"I can convey messages between the divine realms, the underworld, and the world of mortals," Hermes said simply. "I can also escort those I choose."

"Hello, Decanus Arden." Godfree Carrillo saluted. "Good to see you again."

* * *

"I OVERHEARD Hermes talking to Hades about this Yuletide thing they were planning," Godfree explained. The handsome soldier sipped his coffee from a mug, a real cup in his temporarily substantial hands. "I said I knew you. Hermes, in fact, made sure I could reach you on Halloween." He leaned back in his chair and smiled. "You didn't really pay attention to me. What was it? Didn't you believe me?"

Cassandra, Jason's hometown and the most psychic place in the world (according to them), held a Halloween festival every year, which benefited both the town's tourism and the visitors' spiritual inquiries. The festival's grand finale was a visually stunning thinning of the veil between the living and the dead every year.

Godfree, a soldier previously under my command (and one for whom I felt a great deal of guilt about sending to his death), came to see me and told me I was screwing up. That I was ready but chose not to be. That I had to believe before I could lead.

I had no idea what any of that meant.

"It's not that I didn't believe you, Godfree. It's that I don't know what you meant by what you said. Lead what? Lead who? Believe what?" I crossed my arms. "I'm not a soldier anymore.

Okay, whatever this power is that I have to prevent crimes from occurring? It's cool, and I like working for the police department—but they are never going to make me captain." I shrugged. "I just don't know what you were trying to get across."

"Yes, you do."

"Everyone involved in this likes to tell me how I already know what they think I'm supposed to know but that I don't know."

He burst out laughing.

"It's not funny."

"No, you're right, it's not." He nodded, placing his mug down. "You've met four gods today alone, but you appear to be unaffected by the experience. Even though you've looked four gods in the eye, your attitude is exactly the same as when I saw you on Halloween." Godfree pointed. "You're still completely focused on finding a missing panther—"

"Because there's some guy back at my house that claims Athena stole her."

"I doubt Dionysus, Ariadne, Apollo, and Hermes would possibly agree to help out Athena in getting your head on straight, right?" Godfree leaned forward and tilted his head. "You were one of the toughest leaders I ever had in the military.

You could suss out suspects and conspiracies like a dog sniffing out a bone. Yet the longer you're doing this, the more it seems like you're just bouncing from case to case without thinking anything through."

That annoyed me. "I think through the cases. Jeez, Godfree, my entire job is to think through the cases."

"I didn't say cases. Don't dodge the question, Astra."

"I'm not dodging the question," I said, my voice rising involuntarily. "You didn't ask a question. Ask a question, and I'll answer it."

"Okay, let me ask you a question, then."

I glared at him. "What?"

"Why is it that you don't feel like yourself anymore?"

The question brought me up short.

What did the dead know about us that we kept hidden from other people? I couldn't recall saying that out loud to anyone, so it couldn't have been overheard. Yet the question froze my insides like Godfree had hit some emotional bullseye with a spirit arrow.

I realized he was right—though he didn't say enough for me to understand what he understood.

I didn't look at things with a soldier's eye anymore. But I also didn't feel like a soldier, which had been my entire identity for more than a decade. If you aren't a soldier, you may not understand—soldiers do what they do because they feel like they're part of something bigger. It's cliche to say you joined up to be part of something bigger than yourself—and it's a cliche because we all say that a lot. But it doesn't make it any less accurate. We sacrifice out of a sense of duty to something larger than ourselves.

And that was missing now.

I didn't feel that way anymore.

"You always were able to make me think," I told him.

Godfree gave me a half-smile. "I told you on Halloween. You don't have to worship anybody. You don't have to join a religion. But you are a soldier," he said. "I get that you like solving crimes. You like the rush you get when you're able to figure out what's happened. You like that this is giving you a chance to get things done and that your family is suddenly treating you with respect—"

I balked at that. "Hold up. I don't need the respect of my family to feel good about myself, Godfree. I'm not some teenage girl trying to get the approval of my mother." I realized that my voice, without effort or choice, was rising.

He smiled again, and my heart melted a little bit just to see it. "Okay, Pinocchio. Let me just move my chair back, so your nose doesn't poke me."

Archie laughed and then stopped himself.

"You know, I would've made you do push-ups if you talked to me like that when you were alive."

"Hey, Decanus, I have arms," Godfree said, holding up his hands. "How many do you want? Ten? Twenty?"

"Just because you're dead doesn't mean—" I suddenly choked up, my eyes filling with tears. This moment suddenly struck me. Sitting here, talking to him like he'd never died and I'd never lost him—even though I had. I gasped softly as I struggled to catch my breath. "Sorry."

"What are you apologizing to me for? For talking to me like we're old friends?" Godfree leaned forward and grabbed my gloved hands. "You know, I can tell you this now—but I had such a crush on you. There's something about you, this strength that I was so attracted to."

"I was almost ten years older than you!" I told the handsome soldier.

"So what?"

He was young when he died, too young.

Barely a man.

I blinked away the tears again.

Archie sneezed, and his sneeze seemed to break the spell between us.

Godfree released my hands. "Look, I don't really have that long. It's longer than I got at Halloween, and I'm grateful, but it's still not that much time. No use talking about things that are long past and won't ever have the chance to be—though, you know, if you die?" He winked. "Look me up. Differences in ages don't matter all that much in the underworld."

I smiled at him. "I will definitely do that."

"But she won't be dying anytime soon," Archie snapped at Godfree.

"Right." The spectral soldier looked back at me. "Okay, back to it. They are showing you all this so you know it exists. You have met four gods. Four gods from the ancient stories. The siblings of the goddess that gave you your power. You're not taking it seriously enough. You do not understand why the gift was given to you." Godfree looked at Archie. "Either of you."

Archie froze, glaring.

"Are you going to tell me what I need to know? Or are you just the latest in a long line of people who have come to criticize me for my lack of understanding of what I'm supposed to do?" I asked him, gesturing toward Apollo and Hermes. "To be honest, I'm starting to get irritated by everyone telling me I'm not getting what I'm supposed to be getting but then acting like they know and it's a big secret they can't say."

"It's not a big secret." He grinned at me. "Do you want me to tell you?"

I laughed. "You're really starting to annoy me."

"Astra, this is all really simple. Your mother is getting up there in years, and someday, there's going to need to be a new high priestess—"

"Oh, hell, no," I told him, shaking my head. "That is not going to happen. I am not going to be the high priestess—"

"—and that high priestess is going to need a temple guard."

I blinked. "Oh. Okay, so, no one wants me to be a high priestess?" Godfree raised his eyebrow. "Wait a minute. We don't have a temple guard now."

"Of course you do."

"We do not. I live in the 'temple.' I would know if there was a soldier in it."

"Your Aunt Gwennie, Astra. She is by your mother's side all the time," Godfree said, his eyes twinkling with amusement. "Why did you think she lived with all of you?"

* * *

GODFREE AND HERMES LEFT.

"Did you know this?" I asked Archie, pointing my finger at the bird. "Did you know my aunt was the temple guard? Did anyone?"

The owl's expression was strained. Defiantly, he declared, "I have been told that I'm not honest in my answers all the time. And so I want to say that yes, I knew that she was the temple guard because it's my job to know. I'm supposed to know everything." Archie spoke through a closed beak. "But no. I didn't know." He sneezed again. "It seems I didn't know a lot of things."

I pulled my chair closer to Archie and leaned in. "Hey."

He eyed me suspiciously. "What?"

"This is starting to sound like a little bit of a problem for both of us."

"What do you want, a cookie, brainiac?" Archie spat back at me. His big owl eyes widened, and he drew a deep breath as if he was surprised by how quickly the words came out of his mouth. "I apologize for the insulting manner in which I just spoke to you, divine charge Astra," he said in a monotone. "I will try to work on my manner of speech."

I blinked. "Why are you talking like that?"

"Like what, divine charge Astra?"

I pointed. "That. Right there. Why are you talking like that?"

"I. Have. To," he said, his mouth held tightly shut, the words stifled somewhere in his throat. "Just don't ask me. It's part of why I'm in trouble."

I tried to hide a smile. "You're in trouble for being salty?"

"Not as bad as being in trouble for completely rejecting the gods—you know, like you are," he responded sarcastically. The owl froze, eyes wide, and whacked himself in the head with his wing.

"Archie!"

"I know! I know! But I just can't help myself. I've talked this way for several thousand years." He hissed. "I never should have hung out with Euripides. The dude's tongue could slice stone, it was so sharp." Archie looked at me. "And no, I'm not in trouble for being salty. I'm in trouble for not being supportive." He paused. "While being salty."

I leaned back and tilted my head, giving him

the most innocent look I could muster. "Not being supportive of who?"

Archie glared at me with murder in his eyes, and his little owl body vibrated with the pent-up frustration of being unable to tell me off.

"Will I get in trouble for being salty to you?" I asked him.

He stared back, furious. "No."

I contemplated making the most of Archie's predicament and launching a barrage of snarky insults that would crumble the arrogant little owl's self-control. It was only fair, given that the raptor had been telling me for nearly a year how stupid I was. On top of all that, I had to sort through cases while he was away doing whatever divine owls do when they aren't helping.

But I realized that he and I had the same problem—entrenched aspects of our personality that weren't serving us well—and I was concerned for him.

Moreover, he rarely actually hurt my feelings. I'd come to enjoy our sarcastic banter, to be honest with you. And the fact that I didn't have to deal with him constantly on my butt was more of a blessing than a concern.

But I could see how the distance between us had turned into a problem.

A problem that a quarter of the gods on Olympus apparently came out to fix.

"Archie…"

His head jerked to the side, and he blinked at me. "What?"

"I'm not going to take advantage of the fact that you can't snark back at me," I told him. "It sounds like you and I have not been doing the best that we could, and it's not your fault, and it's not my fault. We just fell into a pattern—"

"Actually, it is my fault," Archie said. He paused, then closed his eyes and inhaled deeply, calming himself. When he opened his eyes again, his expression seemed less angry. "Look. I'm not Athena's only owl, and I haven't had a job in thousands of years." He looked slightly embarrassed. "I didn't want you to think I was new at this, and I maybe got a little carried away being back on the human plane."

Archie was a new recruit.

Great.

"That's understandable. And, hey, everyone has to start somewhere, right?" I said cheerfully. "You're still a divine owl, right? And you still know some things that I don't."

"I do." He blinked at me. "You're taking this

better than I thought you would." Archie's face relaxed into what passed for a smile on the owl.

I shrugged. "I'm becoming flexible in my old age." I also knew how to deal with new recruits, but I wouldn't let him know that just yet. I leaned forward. "So what do we do now? Going forward, I mean?"

Archie's face softened, and his brown feathers ruffled out. "We stick together, and I help you," he answered, sounding more sure of himself. "We communicate more. And I stop sneaking off to hang out with the parrots at Parrot Paradise."

I stared at him. "You've been abandoning me to hang out with parrots?"

"Losing some of that flexibility already, huh?" he snapped and then shuddered. "Sorry! Sorry, didn't mean to snap at you. Yes, I have been, Astra. I apologize for doing so. I will no longer do so," he said tensely. Then he exhaled loudly. "This isn't going to be easy."

I reached out, grabbed his talons, and placed him on my shoulder. "I don't think it was meant to be, buddy."

CHAPTER TWELVE

pollo motioned for me to take another seat on the couch before lowering himself into his armchair. Archie, who was riding on my shoulder, leaned in close to my ear and whispered that something had changed.

"I'm sure he knows what we talked about," I replied quietly. "Emma's vampire brother could have heard us talking out there. If he could, I have to believe a god could as well."

"Of course I overheard you," the sun god cheerfully replied. He spread his hands wide as if he had nothing to hide. "If I didn't know when you discovered something about yourselves, this wouldn't be much of a self-discovery journey for either of you."

Was he admitting to having arranged this?

"Self-discovery, huh? When did the Greek gods get into self-help?" Emma asked. "I read a lot of what you guys got up to back in the day, and I don't recall much self-awareness running through the stories."

In Apollo's expression, I noticed a sliver of a smile. "You're remarkably at ease confronting beings far more powerful than yourself. Tell me, do you believe you learned bravery through trials and tribulations or that you were born with it?"

"It's a gift," Emma responded without directly answering the sun god's question.

"And you have a gun," Apollo pointed out.

"A woman of courage never needs weapons, but she may need bail."

Apollo laughed at the quote. "That said, I can assure you that we had a strong sense of self-help! When it came to protection and safety, Sotera was the one to turn to. She aided mortals in discovering their own source of power."

"What kind of spirit is Sotera?" I asked. I mentally raced through all the known spirits I'd been taught about as a child, and I was certain my mother had never mentioned her. "Not a guardian spirit. I learned all of them."

Emma's eyebrows rose. "Are you sure about that?"

"Pretty sure. Why?"

"Sotera was a kind of guardian," Apollo answered. "Well, I mean, I suppose she could be considered a guardian spirit, but really, she was more...more of an inner spirit." He waved his hand as he looked back at me. "You wouldn't know about her. She's not one of the big names, like Sophia or Dike. I'd be surprised if you were taught about her, honestly."

"That makes me feel much better," Emma replied, rolling her eyes.

"What does?" he asked curiously.

"That the Greek goddess of safety is not one of the big names."

Apollo's living room echoed with the bright sound of his laughter. "Like I said, I guess you wouldn't be that familiar with her. Truth is, I never really thought of her as a goddess before." He smiled mischievously. "Maybe I'll have to rethink that. She did have a shrine." He shrugged. "Just one, though."

Emma gave a nod before returning her gaze to mine. "So, what did you discover about yourself?" Her gaze alternated between my owl and me.

Archie and I looked at each other.

"You should probably tell them," the raptor admitted. "I feel like I get in trouble every time I open my mouth." Archie shook his feathers and settled down like a parrot on a pirate's shoulder. "My first lesson is probably to listen more."

We all took seats around the living room looking very much like courteous strangers in a waiting room. In the silence of the moment, the ticking of a grandfather clock behind me became a metronome for my nerves.

"So, I have a confession to make," I said, turning away from the sun god (since he claimed to know everything already) and facing Emma. "I don't know that I disbelieved in the gods' existence so much as I rejected everything that they stood for," I admitted, thinking through my own past reactions as I spoke.

"Talk about your 'six of one, half a dozen of the other.'"

"Do you want to hear this or not?" I asked Emma.

Emma glanced at her phone and then nodded. "Sorry. Go ahead."

"Look, I didn't have to deal with gods of any kind in Imperatorial City. There was no religion in the military. And to be perfectly honest, I liked it. I liked secular society. I resented the hell out of the Olympians for having absolutely no power in this world anymore, but still owning my mother as if they were still who they once were."

"Ouch," Apollo murmured.

"Owning?" Emma asked with a frown.

I shrugged. "As a kid, that's what it seemed like to me. Like they owned her."

"Can your mom not leave Athena's service?" Emma asked, looking taken aback at my phrasing. I understood her reaction, but I couldn't think of any other way to put it. The gods monopolized my mother's focus, her attention, her goals in life. Her daughters were nothing more than additional priestesses for the gods. "Stop being a high priestess if she wants to?"

"I don't know. I never asked. She never would."

"I see."

No, she didn't.

"Well, look at the situation here, right?" I said, pointing to myself and Archie. "I mean, technically, I got a choice about whether or not to take this star power crap on, right? But if I don't do a good job, if I fail, if I change my mind about doing it?" I glanced at the owl. "Archie told me Athena will take my power. And not just the power she gave me, right? The power I was *born* with. Who I am as a witch. Screw up and be stripped of my identity? That feels like being owned." I glared at Archie. "And, by the way, I wasn't told that until after the fact."

At that statement, Apollo turned and stared at Archie, his face so tight I feared it would crack and fall into pieces on the floor. "Archimedes, did you tell her that?" he asked, shocked.

The owl shrank in size as he drew in and nuzzled closer to my hair.

"Are you saying Archie lied to me?" I asked the god.

"Archimedes?" Apollo said sternly in response.

Archie—who had somehow made himself about the same size as an elf owl—stared back at Apollo, his feathers vibrating as he shook. He did not respond.

The god was unmoved and was not giving up on getting an answer. "Did you tell her that Athena would make her mortal if she failed or refused?"

He stared around, eyes bulging in his tiny face as if looking for the nearest exit. Then, finally, the owl looked back at the sun god, his expression blank. "I wasn't given parameters for what I was supposed to tell Astra," he finally responded. "We always used threats back in my day, and so I figured that would work here. Surely you've done it before."

"Cassandra," I coughed.

Apollo looked instantly embarrassed.

As well he should.

Cassandra may well be the first #metoo case in history. Apollo gave her the gift of prophecy and cursed her so her prophecies would not be believed. He did what he did after she withdrew her consent for you-know-what.

"Times have changed," Apollo answered defensively.

"No thanks to the gods, apparently," I pointed out. "So, are you telling me I can just quit doing this whenever I want without consequences?"

"Well, of course, you can just quit, Astra," Apollo responded with a quick shake of his head. "As I said, times have changed, and we have changed." The expression in his eyes was sad, as if he remembered hard lessons learned long ago. "The mortals' god came up with this concept of free will, and it took off across the world like wildfire!"

"Right, but I'm not a human—"

"No, but the energy of this planet shifted from when we ruled. There are many, many, many more humans than there used to be, and their beliefs pressure this place. It exerts pressure on expectations; their desires and demands steer the future, shape the present. As they evolve, you paranormals evolve, and we gods evolve."

"Apparently, Archie was left out of that evolutionary cycle," Emma joked.

"I will ignore you so hard you will start doubting your existence," the tiny owl on my shoulder popped off angrily at Emma's observation. Then he screeched a sound full of self-scorn.

"Jeez, are you okay?"

"You know, if I have to stop insulting people, everyone should have to stop insulting people!" he took a deep breath and peeked out at Emma from under my hair. "I'm sorry," Archie snapped at Emma. Then, under his breath, he muttered, "that you feel that way."

"Well, a non-apology is still sort of an apology, I guess," I joked. I turned back to Apollo. "I just want to ask this again because I want to be really clear. I can change my mind about this, I can quit, and there will be no consequences?"

"That depends on what you mean by consequences," the sun god answered with a kind smile. "Everything we do has consequences. As gods, we have many faces, Astra. And yes, years ago, I was known as a god who punished and destroyed the wicked and overbearing. But I am not that anymore."

"Huh. Why?" Emma asked curiously.

"Because you all do such a bang-up job in punishing yourselves," he answered without elaborating. "The consequence of your quitting, Astra, is that there is no one else quite as suited to the task Athena wishes performed in this area as you. Obviously, that means that if you quit, there will be no one to perform the task." He leaned forward. "But yes, there would be consequences. My entire purpose in meeting you is to show you the consequences."

"The results of what I do?"

"Yes." He held up his hands. "And, I remind you, I was not done."

* * *

"I'M STILL TRYING to figure out if there's an actual panther that's been kidnapped," Emma chuckled. Then, as Apollo rummaged through his kitchen in the other room, Eddie assisting him in cooking dinner, she shifted her position on the couch and grabbed my hand. "How are you doing?"

I blinked. "I don't think you've ever reached out to grab my hand before."

"I don't think I've ever felt so much sympathy for someone," she smirked. "No, that is really not the case. I've seen a lot of things. In Afghanistan, I saw a lot. I had to dig a deeper well of compassion inside my gut just to hold all the sympathy I felt for all the people I came across." She let go of my hand. "You're correct. We haven't really mentioned how we feel about each other, emotions, or anything else."

"I care about you, too," I responded simply.

"And yes, the whole witch thing is cool. The fact that you helped me make more money at work *and* made half of the misogynistic jerks at the precinct afraid of us? Super cool. Like, crazy super cool." She leaned back on the couch. "But I have noticed with the star card stuff, you've struggled with the *why* of it all."

"I never said anything."

"You did. Every time you insulted the gods or claimed they didn't exist."

I sat and thought for a moment. "Yeah. Maybe."

"Not maybe. I noticed other things, too. You don't use the star power much at all. You don't even use your psychometry much—you're much quicker to use your stolen cache of magical military items than anything you inherently possess as a skill. Today when you couldn't see anything in the stable? It's like you were relieved magic didn't work."

"I don't do that," I frowned. Then I thought about past cases, any cases that didn't involve a missing item, and my frown deepened. "Wow. Okay, maybe I do."

"You do. Trust me. You do." Emma reached behind her and grabbed a piece of rabbit jerky, then held it out to the silent, sulking owl. "You know, Archie, you're adorable that size."

The owl was often about two feet tall with a wingspan of at least four feet. Maybe even five feet. Abnormally large, even for an owl. Now, though, he felt small, and his little bird body shrank to match.

If he stood six inches, I'd be surprised.

"I'm glad I'm at least cute since I'm not powerful or brave or honest or wise," he quipped in a small voice, "or insightful or enlightened or knowledgeable—"

"You made a mistake. Everyone makes mistakes," Emma told him, still holding out the rabbit jerky to the tiny owl. "The thing that causes us to evolve, as Apollo mentioned, is that we correct our mistakes. You have the power to change. Obviously, since you've grown to the size of a Barbie doll." She thrust the piece of jerky at him. "Take the treat."

"I'm on a hunger strike," he grumbled.

"What are you protesting?"

"Christmas," he spat. "None of this would be happening if it wasn't Christmas."

I could tell Archie was feeling awkward after Apollo's criticism, and I couldn't blame him for having trouble processing everything that had happened. My day began with me anticipating a massage and possibly a facial. Now I was chasing a mythical panther (who might or might not be real and may very well not be kidnapped) through Palm Beach mansions owned by Greek gods.

"I think I have to finish whatever psychometric journey Apollo plans on taking me on because I honestly have no idea what comes next if I don't," I told Emma. "I don't know what brought all four of us here; if this is about all four of us, if the panther is real, why my sister won't tell me what's going on." I sighed with resignation. "I don't like being led by the nose without any explanation."

"Yeah, but come on, Astra. You were in the

military," Emma joked. "Being ordered to do things you don't understand for ambiguous mission goals that may or may not accomplish anything tangible? That's just a Tuesday for a soldier."

* * *

APOLLO LED me to the dining room. The table was set with fine china and crystal, and the room was scented by massive glass urns filled with red roses. To my right, a gigantic fireplace blazed, its fiery tongues licking at the logs that fed it. The walls were covered in paintings and sculptures with an ancient Greek theme. Above the hearth, a spectacular landscape hung.

Eddie and Emma were already seated, and Apollo pulled out the chair to my right for me. "You look more serene than you did after witnessing Jason's confession of love," he said with a wink. "Processing through stunning information is much faster than we anticipate, isn't it?"

I glared. "No."

"I still want to know what that conversation was about," Emma said to me from across the table. "He must have said something pretty earth-shattering for you to freak out the way you did."

I glared at Emma, knowing that my unwillingness to talk wouldn't be tolerated for much longer. I didn't want to talk about Jason's revelations to his mother, and I still didn't understand why Apollo felt they were necessary.

Eddie cleared his throat. "It doesn't seem like Astra wants to talk about it."

"Eddie is correct," I said. "Astra doesn't want to talk about it."

"Are you talking about yourself in the third person because you think it's cute and witty, or because you're desperately trying to distance yourself from what you saw?" Then, without waiting for me to answer, Emma looked at Eddie and said, "Astra never wants to talk about Jason Bishop, Eddie. That's why it's so much fun pushing her about it."

Apollo poured me a glass of water, and I desperately hoped the clear liquid was a super-sized vodka. "So, Emma, did you and Eddie ever date when you were in Afghanistan?" I asked. "Any steamy nights in a dusty foxhole you want to share?"

"Not cool, Arden." Now it was Emma's turn to glare.

"Thank you all for joining me for dinner," Apollo announced with a friendly smile. "I hope you like Greek food. That," the sun god pointed to a bowl of yellow soup, "is Egg Lemon Chicken Rice soup. Over there we have stuffed cabbage. That's lemon pork with celery. And, of course, spiced walnut cake."

Eddie nodded. "The spiced walnut cake looks wonderful."

"It is!" Apollo turned toward me. "Well?"

I looked around, wondering what I was supposed to do now. "Well, what?"

"Have you decided whether you're going to storm out of here after dinner and go back to Forkbridge, never to think about Greek gods and star power again?" he asked, ladling soup into his bowl. "You now know, for the first time in a year, that you don't have to do any of this. So I assumed that—the storming out—was an option for you."

"It always was an option for me," I responded. "Just because I'd have to pay a penalty for it doesn't mean I wouldn't have done it if I'd wanted to. But I'm not about to storm out." Instead, I grabbed some pork, and my stomach grumbled at the savory scent. "Finish showing me what you have to show me."

"That's wonderful! I knew you'd do the right thing." Apollo smiled at me, and I felt my heart thump in my chest. "I do have a few more things to show you."

"No more Jason."

"Well, we'll see," Apollo said noncommittally.

"You knew she would keep going," Emma said. "I mean, Astra may talk a lot of denial, but she's never backed down from anything."

"I expect that's a prerequisite to be your partner," Eddie said proudly. A barely noticeable flush of pink suffused Emma's cheeks. "That other guy you were partnered up with, the one that didn't want to leave the station to investigate when a football game was on?"

"Oh, he was awful," Emma murmured, eying the walnut cake. "I don't think he realized there was anything else in the world besides football."

"It *was* awful!" Eddie agreed. "I mean, I like football, but you're supposed to be able to do your job, even if you're passionate about football!"

"He was just so bad at the job even when he did it," Emma said. "He didn't seem to realize that bad guys aren't just waiting for you to give them an unfair advantage. They'll actively seek advantage." She rolled her eyes. "The guy was an idiot."

The conversation turned to lighthearted things, safe and meaningless topics, a mundane break in an otherwise confusing day full of revelations that changed everything—and nothing at all.

CHAPTER THIRTEEN

*A*s I previously stated, the ridiculous breeds its own brand of prejudice. I had felt it as I sat in an auditorium listening to a bear shifter lecture me as he declared the end of my career. I might have felt it even more hand in hand with a Greek god past his prime, peering through a swirl of sparkling fog.

"I don't recognize this place," I told Apollo as I gazed out at a...bistro? Steakhouse?

"We're in Baltimore," he responded, again sounding oddly distant. "This seafood restaurant is located on a pier in Baltimore's port, where the Chesapeake Bay meets the Atlantic Ocean."

It appears that merely adding Maryland to Baltimore was too simple.

"Thanks for the geography lesson."

Even though I was only a few feet away from the circular portal viewing window, the air smelled strongly of garlic and fish. Through the restaurant's front window, I could see the moon rise over the bay, and its harbor glittered like a million tiny mirrors. I could hear laughter, shouting, and fanciful music from the docks and restaurants and clubs lining the boardwalk.

"Still not ringing a bell?" Apollo asked. He gestured toward the view. "I believe you know someone here."

A waitress moved to a table where a couple was seated and handed them menus. "It's beautiful, isn't it?" she said. They nodded, watching the moon-rise glimmering off the ripples in the water. "My father's owned this place for almost three decades now, and the dusk never fails to make me catch my breath a little bit."

"Julia," I whispered. "The waitress. That's Julia Rowland."

My old friend's hands were flour-splattered. She was dressed in a white apron with a red bow, her thick, dark hair pulled back in a bun. As she smiled at the couple, she appeared relaxed and at ease.

"Now, this smells delicious," said a man at the next table. He was in his mid-fifties and spoke with a heavy Southern accent as he cut a slice of his fish. The woman with him, who was in her late thirties or early forties, nodded her head in agreement.

"The cook made sure it was made with just a touch of magic," Julia said to the man with a smile and a nod. The man raised his eyebrow. "Bay seasoning! She added just the right amount of bay seasoning." The patron nodded back, looking relieved.

"She looks good. I assume you know all about her life. So tell me—is she happy?" I asked Apollo.

Julia Rowland and I joined the military in the same month, and our paths took us to the same places simultaneously. We happened to be sitting next to each other when Prime Minister Trout Scout announced the dismantling of our department and the deferral of our pensions. Julia and I shared a sleeper car and several bottles of whiskey on our way back to the lives we'd abandoned as eighteen-year-olds.

"Yes," he said, sounding surprised. "She was born to be here. This is a place where your friend feels at home, and her family is thrilled to have her back."

"So, is this some sort of message that what we did in the military wasn't what we were supposed to do? She was supposed to fry fish, while I was supposed to stay at home and work in the new age store?"

"One of the best desserts I've ever tasted," an older man at another table said. "Julia, you're an angel, and your pie could put a smile on anyone's face."

"Of course not," Apollo said, gesturing toward the portal and changing its focus. "If she'd stayed here and never gotten her military training, could she have done that?" The opening turned, shifted, and drew up on a framed article hung prominently on the wall.

LOCAL WOMAN RESCUES HUMAN TRAFFICKING VICTIMS

"Julia—like you—made off with her fair share of Ministry tools," Apollo explained with a soft chuckle. "The Periculum Indicator was one of the items she grabbed. It pointed to a boat in the marina just south of here, where several women were held. Julia rescued them by pretending to deliver dinner to the 'incorrect' boat, after which she gave a resounding thumping to the men holding the women."

"Damn, good for her," I said quietly. "And,

frankly, I'm a little jealous. I really wanted to snag one of those. Tried to get one before I left, but the shelf was empty."

The Periculum Indicator was a small stone that glowed if there was a threat nearby. Since it was magic, it didn't necessarily just mean a danger to the bearer of the stone—it was enchanted and tuned to problems a mile out from itself in any direction. Its real power was in its ability to direct the stone's owner to the victim's location. In the military, it was used for kidnappings and hostage situations.

"So why are we here?" I asked Apollo.

"I don't know, Astra. Why don't you tell me?"

The scene shifted before I could respond as the fog grew thicker.

* * *

A WOMAN in a bright blue dress and red lipstick stood facing the cashier. "I hope your daughter really likes the blue calcite sphere. We don't get a lot of those in, you know, so it's pretty rare."

I recognized the voice, and as the fog lifted and the portal opened, I realized the cashier was my sister, Ami. Even though this was a new age witchy store, my sister was dressed in a red velvet ankle-length dress and a white fur hat. She looked like a Christmas-flavored witch.

Blue dress woman looked dubious. "And you're sure it will work?"

"Blue calcite is a gentle stone to use while recuperating, clearing negative emotions, and encouraging rest and relaxation, which aids in physical healing," Ami responded, nodding. "I think it'll be just what she needs."

"You've never steered me wrong before," the woman responded, nodding. She handed Ami her credit card to pay. "Are you making plans for Christmas?" The woman looked concerned. "Do I say Merry Christmas to you, or is that intolerant?"

"Merry Christmas to you, too! It's never intolerant to offer someone good wishes, I would think. It's not my holiday, true—but I like it just the same," Ami responded cheerfully, ringing up the crystal ball and handing it—and the credit card—to the woman. "There you go. Enjoy! Have a wonderful holiday, Mrs. Bertram!"

My sisters Ayla and Althea entered as Mrs. Bertram was leaving.

"Is there anyone here?" Ayla inquired as she sat down on the stool.

"Nope. We're on our own unless ghosts are

lurking around or Archie is hidden away in a box somewhere."

I watched the three of them settle around the counter, leaning in like they were about to hold a secret meeting. Then, finally, Ami glanced toward the door, nodded, and then whispered, "How do you think Astra's doing?"

"I haven't heard anything. But Mom and Aunt Gwennie have been locked in that room with Alexarchos for the last hour," Ayla said, shrugging. "That room is warded against sound and ghosts, so I haven't been able to find out a thing."

"It doesn't feel right, not being able to help her," Ami said with a sigh.

"Who, Astra? Lest you all forget, she did just fine without our help for thirteen years," Thea said with a shrug. "She'll figure out what's going on sooner or later."

"Maybe we should just send a text. Tell her hi. Ask how she's doing. You know, just generally," Ayla said, pulling out her phone. "He didn't tell us we shouldn't talk to Astra. Just not talk to her about what he said."

My eyes narrowed. Who's he? Apollo? Hermes? Alexarchos?

Thea swatted Ayla's phone down. "Don't you dare. He was super clear."

"Who's *he*? Are they talking about you?" I asked the sun god.

He didn't respond.

Because of course he didn't.

"Why do you think everyone is making such a big deal about whether or not Astra believes certain things?" Ayla asked her older sisters. "No one asked what she believed before, so why does it matter now?"

"My guess? She's found her way home—that's why," my sister Althea responded. "She's come back to where her power is, where she belongs. She's reconnected the lines that were cut when she left and on top of that? Now she's stronger than she's ever been."

"But everybody has checks and balances." Ami shrugged. "We're that for each other, right? So, look—all three of us are connected to the ancient gods, and they are connected to each other. That means each of us has a piece, and each of our pieces connects us to the others. You understand?"

Ayla did not look like she understood. "So, you're saying that Astra has to find her piece, too?" Ayla asked, sitting up straight. Ami and

Althea laughed. "What? Why are you laughing? I hate it when you guys laugh at me."

"Sorry," Ami said. "I don't mean it in a bad way. It's just that Astra always had her piece of it, her tie. We all do. It's something inherently within us because of who we are."

"Yep." Thea nodded to Ami. "It's something within all of us."

"*If that which thou seekest thou findest not within thee, then thou wilt never find it without thee,*" Ayla said, quoting one of the sacred texts. She looked at her older sisters expectantly.

Ami and Althea nodded.

"Exactly," Thea said, smiling. "Astra doesn't have to join the coven or change her beliefs or whatever. But I think the gods have gotten a little sick of her denying what makes her what she is."

"So they're punishing her?"

"No, Ayla," Ami told my youngest sister, shaking her head. "The gods aren't punishing her. This isn't a punishment. They're giving her a gift." Ami leaned forward, her chin on her hands. "What's the ancient Greek saying that Mom made sure to pound into our heads as we grew up? The one she said was more important than—"

"Know thyself," Ayla interrupted.

"Right. It was on Apollo's temple. It was

quoted in Sun Tzu. It was an answer given in *The Spirits Book.* The Wachowskis even used one of the Latin versions as the inscription over the Oracle's kitchen doorway in their *Matrix* movies," Thea told Ayla. "It's an ancient truth, a universal truth, that transcends time and belief systems and religions and cultures."

"When Astra got kicked out of the military, she lost a part of herself. Well," Ami said, tilting her head, "at least I think she thinks she did."

"But it's still there," Thea said. "What we are is always within us."

"The gods are just helping her find it again," Ayla said, nodding.

They vanished as the fog grew thicker and swirled.

* * *

"OKAY, I GET THE POINT," I told Apollo. A desolate landscape was revealed as the fog lifted. A white and blue-robed figure stood in the distance as if it were waiting for something. A glow emanating from the figure's skin illuminated the swirling wisps of fog that surrounded it.

"Do you?" Apollo asked kindly. "I don't sense that you do."

"Yeah, well, I don't recall you having awesome intuitive instincts, dude." The Greek gods were not omniscient or omnipotent or omnipresent in the myths. They each had strengths and weaknesses—and I didn't recall Apollo's strength being empathy or intuition. "Did you sense that Euripides would paint you as a fiendish monster? Or that punishing a woman for not having sex with you would, a few thousand years forward, make you look like a completely abusive a—"

"Hello?" the man in the robe called out. He stepped forward. "Is anyone here?"

Then again, I didn't recall Apollo being able to zip people around like this, either. There were numerous special abilities he possessed, such as foresight into the future and control over light. He also could heal and inflict disease on others. In addition, Apollo was a deadly marksman with a bow and arrow in combat.

Teleportation?

Not a peep.

"Halt!" A voice boomed out of the fog, which now seemed to be everywhere. I scanned the horizon but couldn't see who was speaking. It was as if the entire vista was the source of the overwhelming voice. "Who goes there?"

The robed figure came closer, and the light

from his body softened and grew dim. "I'm Bob Robbins," he responded, his head swiveling on his neck as he searched for the questioner. "I come in peace? I dunno, man, I don't know how I got here, to tell you the truth. One minute I was with my boys robbing a store, and the next—"

"What is the nature of your visit to this place?" the voice asked. "What is your one desire? The one thing you wish above all else?"

Bob seemed taken aback by the weight of the question, but he answered seemingly without thinking. "I am looking for my family," he responded, glancing back behind him. "I need to find my family. My wife, my kid."

"You are looking for your family?" the voice repeated. "But they are not dead. You are dead. You have crossed over. You have left them."

Bob seemed dumbstruck with the knowledge of his own passing, and for a moment, he looked like he couldn't breathe. Then, finally, he choked out, "Look, I screwed up, okay? I get it. I need to change my life. This is, like, one of those near-death experiences, right?" Bob suddenly looked angry. "Okay, I get it. Send me back."

"I cannot," the voice responded sadly. "You have finished your life."

"No!" he cried out. "I am not ready to die! I

have more to do! I can't leave my wife, my kid!" He ran forward and craned his neck toward the sky, shouting, "I have unfinished business, I have responsibilities!"

"You have no responsibilities left," the voice responded. "Any responsibilities you left undone will be taken up by someone else now. You have finished everything you were capable of doing." The voice was calm and serene, but the traveler seemed shaken—as if he could feel the truth of its words.

"Please," he cried, tears streaming down his face. "Please, no—I was capable of so much more! That can't be all I was! I can't leave things like that!"

"You can't go back," said the voice. "You are no longer alive. You are dead. And what you did was what you were capable of. Because you did only what you did, and you never did anything more, and you made it your truth. One's duty to oneself, others, and the gods has been fulfilled as much as it will ever be. Who you were in life is who you are in death."

"But I could have done more!"

"Naturally, you could have. However, you were unaware of this or did not believe it and thus did not. That knowledge is the hell with which you will have to live for eternity unless you try again and do things differently."

Damn.

Harsh.

Watching him cry, we saw him fall to his knees, muffling his cries with his hands while weeping. He wept for a long time before finally becoming silent and gazing up at the sky with his now dry and red-rimmed eyes.

"I'm sorry," he whispered.

"Everyone always is if they wasted their life," the voice responded sadly.

The fog thickened and swirled around me. "You have seen what few get to see, Astra Arden," the booming voice said as the plateau faded from view. "Always remember: Don't be like Bob."

* * *

APOLLO DROPPED MY HAND.

"Those are lessons that should be easy to remember," Apollo said, smiling.

"What lessons?" Emma asked.

"'Know thyself' and 'Don't be like Bob,' I think," I told her. I closed my eyes and imagined walking through the pearly gates only to be greeted by a judgmental voice telling me I had no chance to make amends for anything I'd done. Even though it was evident to me that Bob had committed a crime, I felt terrible for him as he faced the finality of his life and a bucketful of regret.

"Don't forget 'have dinner with the middle school teacher,'" Apollo added.

I blinked open my eyes and stared at him.

"Who's Bob?" Eddie asked, confused.

"Someone that just died and didn't do what he should have with his life, apparently." I walked over to the couch, sat down, and held out my hand to Archie—who was still a tiny little elfin owl. "Apollo took me to see the woman we helped when we first met. Then Jason, who confessed some deep feelings for me," I said, ticking off the visions. "The second trip, we visited a friend from the military, Julia. Then back at home, to eavesdrop on my sisters discussing this whole thing. And then we went to...purgatory? The afterlife? The underworld?"

Apollo just stared, not confirming or denying anything.

"What did it look like?" Archie asked.

"It was gray, barren, misty, and foggy," I told him.

"The underworld," Archie said, nodding.

"Sounds like the place people go before they get shipped to Elysium or Tartarus. It's pretty gray and barren."

"So, wait—those places are real for everybody?" Emma asked, her face shocked. "Heaven and hell aren't real?"

"It's more complicated than that," Apollo told her.

"Okay," Emma said, clearly waiting for a further explanation on the intricacies of a multicultural, multi-religious afterlife. "It's more complicated than that?"

"Glad you agree," the sun god said with a nod.

Emma blinked. "Yeah, no, that was kind of a question—"

"And there's only one way you will truly get a definitive answer," Apollo said, his kind face turning stern and cold. "How bad do you want that answer, Emma Sullivan?"

Emma did not respond right away. Instead, her mind appeared to be blazing through the benefits and drawbacks of various answers—or, more likely, attempting to find a way to trick the sun god's answer without, you know, dying. "I guess I can wait," she finally said, looking disappointed.

I pulled out my phone and typed in 'Bob Robbins obituary.'

Huh.

He was real.

And he was dead.

Robert Xavier Robbins, 33, was killed three days earlier when he and two other men attempted to rob a mom-and-pop convenience store. Bob was shot in the back, unaware the proprietor's wife was in the storeroom and in possession of a gun they kept by the safe. Bob was declared dead at the crime scene and survived by his wife and three-year-old son.

I read the obituary to everyone.

"Sounds like good riddance," Eddie said with a dispassionate coldness.

"Dude. There's a three-year-old that will grow up without a father," I told him. "Maybe you don't know what that's like, but I do."

"He'll grow up without a criminal for a father," Eddie countered. "That's a win in my book."

"Okay, before we get into an argument, why were you shown all this stuff, Astra?" Emma asked, glancing at the sun god. "I mean, what was the purpose?"

I understood what Apollo was trying to say. I mean, I'd have had to be a moron not to—I hadn't wanted to return home in the first place. While I loved my family, I felt disconnected from them in some ways. A little distant. Unwilling to commit fully. The same could be said for the abilities I was given—as well as the owl who was supposed to be my constant companion.

Though, to be fair, some of that responsibility rested on him.

But still.

I did just enough to say I was doing my duty. Fulfilling an obligation.

But that's it.

I wasn't particularly invested in anything other than keeping my mom off my back, being friendly with my sisters, and teaching them a thing or two. I wasn't as enthusiastic as Julia when she served crabs to tourists in Baltimore. I wasn't a criminal like Bob, but I'd stepped outside the lines to solve cases.

If I was honest, I wasn't the best version of myself at the moment.

And if I kept that honesty going, I knew why.

Partially because I felt I had left the best version of myself in the military, and partly because the resentment over where I had landed had been swallowed, buried, ignored—but was not entirely gone.

"The purpose, I think, is that I have the ability to be better," I told her. "More present. More honest. More connected. I could do more at the shop, do my job better, and care more. I could teach my sisters things they'd never learn anywhere else." I shrugged. "But I don't. I still have one foot and half my head in the military. In my old life. Mourning it, I guess."

"You could figure out why Athena gave you her sister's power," Archie added quietly. "And explore what you can do with it."

I looked at Archie. "Yep. You're right. I could."

Emma watched me. "But?"

"But nothing. They're right. I have to do better."

Apollo's eyes widened with excitement. "This has been a successful session, then! Thank you so much for stopping by. I don't get to do enough of these, you know."

"I still have one more question, though."

"Of course." Apollo looked eager to dispense more wisdom. "What can I help with? I'm good at many things, you know."

I crossed my arms, glaring at the self-congratulatory sun god. "Is there a freaking panther or not?"

CHAPTER FOURTEEN

ortunately, there was, according to the sun god, a panther.

Unfortunately, Apollo was only willing to tell me that. He wished us luck, confirmed we enjoyed our meal and led us to the door like he was late for another appointment.

"That was, without a doubt, the weirdest afternoon I've ever spent anywhere," Emma said as we walked down the backyard pathway toward the beach. "Though, you know, I say that now, but we've had weirder afternoons. I guess I say that pretty often, now that I'm thinking about it." She glanced at me. "You have to admit this is way more fun than a massage, though."

"I absolutely do not have to admit that, no," I responded abruptly.

"Okay, maybe it wasn't fun, but it was probably useful. Look at it this way, you just got, like, six months of therapy in an afternoon," she quipped. "You and the owl both."

"I would've preferred a massage," Archie told Emma from his perch on my shoulder. "Or a letter from Athena with bullet points. Simple. Fast. To the point. That would've accomplished—"

"Why would Apollo have a picture of Alexarchos in his house?" the werewolf asked, opening the gate for the two of us and cutting off Archie's observation.

"You told him?" I asked, wondering how Eddie knew.

Emma nodded once. "Yeah, I explained while you were meditating or whatever. I don't know that it's that weird, though, right? They're all connected to the Olympians in one way or another. Well," she mused. "most *are* the Olympians."

Eddie made a low, gruff sound, like the ones dogs make when they're frustrated. "I don't know much about the gods. Werewolves don't deal with them. But it seems odd to me that there would be a picture of another god's priest at Apollo's house."

"You guys would know about that more than I would," Emma said as we stepped back out onto the pristine private sand beach. "But I can say the two of them looked like they were pretty close in that photo. I mean, it almost looked romantic."

"It's certainly possible. Apollo doesn't reach Dionysus-level sexual adventurousness, but no one could call the sun god conservative," I mused out loud. "Look, considering everything we learned at Apollo's, I'd like to go back and take another look at the panther's stable. We had less information when we first looked at it." I squinted down the dark beach. "Something about it is nagging at me, and I'm not sure what it is."

It was too clean and too empty.

As the afternoon unfolded, I'd wondered what I might have missed since, at the time, I didn't realize just how much of this little Palm Beach road trip might have been staged as an intervention for Archie and me.

I looked around. The sun had set for the day, and the sky above us was clear and dark, lit dimly by its last hot blaze. Yet, despite the beauty of the sunset, we were the only people on the beach for what seemed like miles.

Granted, there weren't many people on the beach when we arrived this afternoon, but it was early in the evening. I was surprised it was so isolated.

"What's wrong?" Emma asked. "You have that look."

I looked at my watch. "It's only seven o'clock. Not that late." I gestured to the right and left of where we stood. "Where is everyone?"

The wind blew from the south. The beach wasn't cold by most standards, and the warmer wind kept the evening chill out of the air. Despite it being pretty comfortable outside, the beach all these people fought so hard to keep for themselves wasn't in use by anyone other than us.

"It's harder to find a place to park in the evening for folks that don't live here," Eddie said with a shrug. "The people that live here? They don't come out much at night." He looked around the expensive homes. "A lot of them are probably vacationing in Europe or on an African safari or at some house they own somewhere else."

"Why do you live here amid this bourgeoisie hellscape with raked sand and signs keeping people off?" I asked Eddie, curious. "What was it about Palm Beach that attracted you?"

"The bourgeoisie?" Eddie asked, looking confused.

"Stinking rich people with stinking rich stuff," Emma told him.

He nodded like he understood. "It's been meticulously developed over the years, so the town itself is just beautiful—though I guess that's a matter of opinion." Eddie looked around and smiled faintly. "I don't know. I just like the small-town character."

"They bought and paid for the small-town character," I murmured.

"Mixed in with the ability to hobnob with titans of industry," Emma added with a snort. "I think you're hoping to be picked up on someone's staff. Become the private security for the CEO of Peroosal or Oaks and Crows, maybe?" For years, the two national companies—a tech company and a department store—had their main executives living in Palm Beach. The two men were notorious for their appalling sense of greed. "I'm sure it pays way better than a detective's salary."

I stopped my thoughts from running off in the direction of Renzo and his future private security career. "You know what? Forget I asked. Can we bring the focus back to what we're doing here?"

"Do we even know what we're doing here?" Archie asked, his beak clicking softly in my ear.

"I'm going to give you a pass on that snark because we did get a little sidetracked." Archie's beak clicked again, but he didn't respond. "There are a few things we know at this point. First, obviously, there was a conspiracy to get me here to Palm Beach so I could take a trip down memory lane with the sun god in there. Second, my family knows about it, and it must've been at the direction of Athena because it involved Archie."

"Why did it have to involve Athena?" Emma asked.

"Archie is Athena's owl," Eddie told her. "There's no way the other gods would've lectured him the way they did if Athena hadn't given her permission." And he glanced at me. "I may not know much about the gods, but I know that much. It would've had to be at her direction."

"You know, I'm sitting right here," the owl grumbled. "You could just ask me."

"You heard what I said," Eddie told him. "You could just join in the conversation like anybody else."

Archie glared. "You're correct, fine sir." The owl's voice was irritated, and he was clearly fighting back the insult I would've expected to accompany that expression on his face. "I shall endeavor to participate more fully in the future."

"I think I liked him better the other way," Emma said.

Archie grimaced in annoyance.

I pulled out my phone and checked my texts in case Ami had changed her mind and decided to pass me information, but her last message of luck stared back at me. "They have to know. There's no way they would just not bother with a response if we were actually in danger." I looked up. "Okay, we're not getting anything done standing on this beach," I said, slipping my phone back in my pocket. "Let's go back to Pantera's cell."

"Wait a minute."

Emma and I looked at Eddie.

"What if that's not a name?" Eddie asked, his expression confused.

With a disappointed exhale, Emma turned toward Eddie. "What do you mean?"

"Well, Pantera is literally just panther in Italian. Not just Italian, though. Galilean, Portuguese... Who said that was the panther's actual name?"

"Alexarchos, the butler Birch back there at

Dionysus's house, my mother," I responded. "They all made it pretty clear the panther was female, and they called her by the name Pantera. Or, to be more exact, they use the word pantera as if it was her name."

Eddie looked like he was thinking this over.

"Come on. Out with it. Why does the panther's name matter?"

"It's not so much that it matters what the name is," Eddie said, leaning against Apollo's beachfront fence. "But...okay, look. For shifters, we often talk about our inner-animal like it's a separate being. We give it a name, and, to be frank, sometimes the names aren't that creative. For example, my inner wolf is named Lupa." He looked at us both. "That's Italian for wolf."

"No," Emma broke in. "Lupa is Italian for a *female* wolf. You're male."

Eddie nodded. "I know. Some of us have inner animals that are the same gender, and some move across genders." He shrugged. "I couldn't really tell you why, and I can't really explain it to you. It's not something I can put into words very easily. But when I change and go full-wolf?" He shrugged. "I'm a female."

Emma stared at Eddie as if she'd never seen him before.

Again.

I waited for my usually glib friend to make a funny comment or ask intrusive questions, but she just kept staring. Finally, I spoke. "You think the panther we're looking for could be a shifter?" I asked.

He nodded. "It's a possibility. Pantera could be nothing more than the name for someone's inner-panther."

"Ayla said Pantera was just panther in Latin."

Eddie shook his head. "She's not correct. *Panthera* is panther in Latin."

"Pantera is a heavy metal band," Emma added, nodding.

"Do we think the heavy metal band is the missing panther?" I asked her. "Or that their music has something to do with the missing panther?"

"Well, no, but—"

"Then stop bringing up the band."

"Rude," she muttered.

The werewolf rolled his eyes and pulled out his phone. After tapping on the screen for a bit, he said, "Pantera is panther in Italian, Polish, Romanian, Spanish... And Portuguese. Well, Brazilian Portuguese. Possibly even more." He held up the phone. "That's just what I was able to find in a few minutes."

I nodded. "Okay, so what does this mean?"

We all looked at each other, waiting for one of us to point out the pertinent information in the etymology discussion we had just had. Instead, everyone remained deafeningly silent, looking around with anticipation.

"Great. So all we got out of that was that the panther *could* be a shifter?" I asked, raising my eyebrow. The two of them nodded. "We're not the finest LEO minds ever to take on a case, are we?"

"Well, to be fair, you were on a psychic tour with the sun god all day, and we had to sit and wait for you," Emma pointed out defensively. "So we're a little behind."

I exhaled. "Yeah, no, I get it. Didn't mean to sound judgy."

"You did, a little bit." Emma shrugged. "Apology accepted."

I looked at her. "I didn't apologize."

"But you should have, Astra," Emma said and winked. "I was just saving you the trouble and cutting to the chase."

"Fine, I'm sorry for insulting our collective intelligence," I told her. "You'd think with our collective magic and ties to the Olympians, we wouldn't be traipsing around on a beach at Christmas trying to determine if there even is a panther to begin with, but here we are."

"As long as we don't get waylaid by the ghost of Christmas future, we should be able to get back on track," Emma told me, her voice confident. "We'll figure it out, Astra."

"Okay. Let's head back to Dionysus's place," I said, pointing. "At least there's booze there."

* * *

"Obviously, there is a panther. It is normally located here, but it is no longer located here," Birch said as he walked us back toward the big house from the stable. "From all those things you just told me, how did you come to believe there was no panther?" he stopped, turned, and looked at me following my explanation regarding where we'd been and what we had been doing. "To be honest, why would you believe you are so significant or noteworthy that this was all solely part of some elaborate conspiracy to get you down here?"

"Do the Greek gods engage in anything other than elaborate conspiracies? I mean, really— their entire historical existence is basically one long, complicated revenge fantasy. Their victims are usually some dude walking by who stepped wrong. Right?" Emma asked him. When he didn't answer, she laughed. "Come on. That was funny."

Birch didn't laugh.

"Wasn't that kind of funny?" she asked me.

Eddie watched but said nothing.

"It was a conspiracy just to get me down here, at least on Apollo's part." Birch stared at me with a no-nonsense glare. "He more or less admitted it. Now, it doesn't necessarily mean there's no panther, and it doesn't consequently mean even if there is a panther that the panther isn't missing."

"How generous of you."

I frowned. "Birch, right now, I think you're all suspicious, and you may all be in on it. You could make this way easier on me by just telling me exactly what's going on here."

"If you don't even know whether there is a panther, it sounds like you don't know a whole lot of information," Birch responded in a tone tight with impatience. He glanced at Archie and smirked. "And your divine animal seems to have lost some of its stature. Perhaps instead of feasting with Apollo like spoiled children and peeking through the mists, you should have been looking for the panther you've been charged to find."

Before I could respond, Emma's words came out like a cracked whip.

"Hey, dude, it's your panther, you know. It's not our panther. The only reason we came down here was to head off some kind of multi-god Florida heavy drama war between Athena and Dionysus, and what we *have* learned indicates that might never have really been a concern for anyone," Emma told the butler in a sharp but unconcerned voice. "The way I see it, our concerns aren't really our concerns anymore. And your concerns?" Emma shrugged. "They aren't necessarily our concerns—unless we choose to make them our concerns. So maybe cut the insults out."

I blinked.

Oh, snap.

She was right.

Well, *maybe* she was right.

Like I mentioned on the beach, if my family knew what was going on here and weren't helping, I likely wasn't in any real danger. But it also probably meant they weren't in any danger, either.

Didn't it?

The butler's head jerked forward. "You're awfully ballsy for a mortal standing in a god's home."

Emma stepped forward as if to prove to Birch she wasn't afraid of him or anyone else. "Yeah, well, I have a werewolf to my right and a witch to my left that Greek gods go through a hell of a dance to persuade to their side, so I'm feeling kinda cocky at the moment." She reached forward and brushed some nonexistent fluff off his lapel. "I'd also probably prefer to be driving around Palm Beach and seeing the rich people's Christmas lights as opposed to trying to grab a nonexistent panther by the tail."

"Back up," Birch said, his tone low.

Emma took one step back and stared.

"While that may be true for you, Detective Sullivan, the missing panther is still my concern," Eddie Renzo said, his deep voice wrapped in the tenor and tone of a police officer once again. "There have been multiple complaints about that panther running free—so one does exist. It needs to be found. I don't want anyone in Palm Beach to get hurt—or, frankly, the animal to be injured." He raised his eyebrow. "If it can be injured, in any case."

"Well, that's true," Emma said and then

yawned loudly. "Before we go check out the stable again, I have a question for you, Birch. The panther—is it a shifter?"

Montgomery Birch flushed and cleared his throat. "Why would you ask me that?"

Well.

That wasn't an answer.

Emma narrowed her eyes. "She's a witch, and he's a werewolf. I'm sure you're *something* not mortal. There are two gods in that house; there's another god a few houses down. So, maybe the better question is, why would you avoid answering the question? I mean, we're all pretty open about who and what we are, yes?"

"I haven't been authorized by my employers to answer any of your questions," the butler said. He pushed himself off the fence and walked toward the stable. "If you follow me, I am authorized to take you into the stable."

"What is he?" Emma asked me as we followed again.

"Who, Birch?"

She nodded. "Is he a god, a demigod, a shifter, a witch?"

I shrugged. "Honestly, he seems mortal to me."

Eddie Renzo sniffed. Loudly.

Montgomery Birch was not far enough away

for this to be a private conversation, but if he overheard us, he contributed no information about his identity.

"Have you noticed?" Archie whispered.

As soon as the words left his mouth, I did.

The groups of revelers that had dotted the property were no longer there. Like the beach, it was now quiet and empty. "Where did everyone go?" I asked the butler as we approached the outer building's door. "The fires at the fire pits are no longer burning. It's quiet. Normally, I would just think the party was over, but this is Dionysus's house, so that doesn't make sense."

"Here you are," Birch said, unlocking the door. He pulled it wide, turned, and walked swiftly back toward the main house. "I'll be back when you're done."

I watched him go and wondered…how, exactly, would he know when we were done?

* * *

A HALF HOUR LATER, I punched the wall. "I don't see anything different than I saw before." The images I'd seen with Apollo through the swirling fog and mist were a hundred times clearer than any of the images I was getting inside this building. "Something is blocking me, and I don't know what it is. Hey, Archie," I said, turning to look for the raptor. "You have any ideas?"

The owl perched on a ceiling beam and peered down at us. "The same thing I've been telling you since I showed up," Archie said and flapped. "Use the Astraea power that Athena gave you. If you're right, and this is all just a big mystery play to get you closer to who you were meant to be?" he tilted his head. "That's the key. I mean, obviously."

"Hey now. I heard a little bit of sass in that last sentence, bird," Emma warned him.

I leaned against the wall and crossed my arms. "You can still hear Archie," I pointed out, drumming my fingers against my arm impatiently. "You can only hear him when we have a star card case. The Apollo card. The Apollo card is the card that flipped." I said it aloud, though I was mostly talking to myself. "So, who is in jeopardy? Who are we supposed to guard? Is there anyone, or can you hear Archie because Athena wants you to?"

"Oh my gosh," Emma said, staring at me.

"What? Did you just think of something?"

"No, but you did just say something about Athena, and you didn't say anything insulting or denigrating after it." Emma smiled, raising a bushy eyebrow. "That's progress. I guess even the sharpest edge will go blunt if you beat it against a brick wall long enough."

"Har har."

"Unfortunately, your readjusted attitude doesn't get us any closer to figuring this out." I nodded slowly, acknowledging her point. "What do you think?"

"Hey, Archie, when we first got here, you said you thought Athena took the panther," I reminded him, craning my neck up to the rafters. "Why did you say that? What made you think Athena took the panther?"

"Well, I don't *know* that Athena took the panther, like snuck in here and stole it," Archie said, walking toward me on the beam. "And by the way, it took you long enough to ask me that question."

"We sliding back toward snarky?" I called up cheerfully.

The goddess's very own owl stopped walking, and I could hear his talons digging into the wood. He blinked, flapped his feathers, and sighed. "Ugh. Fine. You're right. I apologize," Archie told me with exaggerated solemnity. "I came in here through the window at the top." He jerked his head toward a small square window in the arched roof. "When I came in, I could smell Athena."

"You could smell her?" I frowned. "What does that mean?"

"Her scent. I smelled myrrh and roses."

"I'm sorry, did you say murder and roses?" Eddie shouted up from across the open room. "I couldn't quite hear you."

"Myrrh! Myrrh!" He flapped his wings in aggravation. "You know, like frankincense and myrrh? You need to clean out your ears, Wolf! I thought you were supposed to have sensitive hearing?"

"Higher pitches, not much better hearing," Eddie told Archie.

"Wait a minute, you can understand my owl?" I asked the detective, stunned.

"Well, of course I can—wolves are sacred to Athena, too. Actually, wolves are sacred to several gods. We're kind of popular." Eddie looked at me oddly. "Didn't you know that?"

"The things I don't know about the gods and what's sacred to them could probably fill a book." I gave him a look I hoped reflected my regret at not knowing as much as he did about the gods and my annoyance at him for bringing it up again.

"It's also probably *in* a book," Archie popped off from above. "You know, that you could *read*."

"How did I not notice you could understand him?" I muttered, glaring up at Archie. "You're backsliding, by the way."

Archie stared back at me and deadpanned, "I can't slide. I'm an owl."

"That's two," I told him, holding up two fingers.

"Three, really," Emma said. "You're forgetting about the one before."

"Oh, get a grip, you two. That was just funny. That's not an insult."

"You've been kind of distracted today," the werewolf told me, coming back to the previous conversation. "Don't worry about it."

"As much as I enjoy watching all of this cheerful banter," Emma said with forced enthusiasm, "we really do need to figure out where this panther is. I know your thing with Apollo kind of distracted us, and it *was* important —but we do have some kind of star card thing going on, and we don't even know whose life is in danger. But, unfortunately, since I can still hear the bird, I have to assume we haven't done what we need to do."

"I repeat: use your Astraea power," Archie said again.

"Okay, brainiac. Great idea." I held up my hands. "What do I do, O sacred gift from Athena? Aren't you supposed to tell me what I'm supposed to do?"

Archie cleared his throat. "Astraea was the virgin goddess of justice, innocence, purity, and precision—"

"Virgin goddess, huh?" Emma said with some amusement. "Jason Bishop's going to be *really* disappointed to hear about that, huh?"

"Emma, shut up," I snapped, pulling off my gloves. "Archie, what do I do?"

The bird ruffled his feathers. "Break whatever enchantment is blocking the memories of this room. That would be my suggestion," the owl responded thoughtfully. "We need to know if this panther is real or just some construct the gods came up with to make us run around in the directions they wanted us to go."

I nodded and lifted my hands.

"Wait!" Emma shouted.

I lowered my hands.

"We're going to step outside in case you, you know, set the place on fire or something," Emma said, pointing toward the door. "While you're in here doing this? I'm going to text your sister Ami and see if I can find out anything else about the Apollo card and what she was doing a reading on. Maybe if it's not you, she'll answer me. I'm already an Athena believer."

I nodded. "Sounds like a plan."

"I'm going with them," Archie told me. He paused and looked down at me. "You can do this, Astra. I know that you can. It's a god's power. There's no special trick to it. You tell it what you want, and you believe it can do it. And then you let it do what you need to do."

"It all sounds so simple," I told him.

"It does. But it's not. Your belief is key." He skittered toward the square window and jumped up into it. Before he left, he leaned back in and stared into my eyes. "Good luck."

"Thanks."

In the sudden quiet of the room, I thought I smelled myrrh.

"Okay," I whispered, raising my arms again. "Here we go."

CHAPTER FIFTEEN

*D*espite Archie's wild claims of my ultimate control over the Astraea power (and his newly supportive tone, which didn't entirely fit him), using the Astraea power was not as straightforward and easy as he claimed.

Yes. I know what you're thinking.

The answer is yes.

Despite all the problems I'd had up until now —problems around me and some that I admittedly caused myself—I really thought it would be so simple to do.

At my core, I'm really a confident optimist.

I know, shocker.

Anyway, I was sure I'd get it. No problem.

I mean, it was just starlight magic, right?

I closed my eyes and imagined the night sky. The heavens. I pictured shooting stars and distant galaxies, all dense with trillions of points of light. I attempted to feel the magic within myself. As I imagined it, an unnatural sound hummed in the air, like a crackling radio. I felt the energy build and build and build and then…

Nothing.

Whatever I felt sputtered out like an engine that just ran out of gas.

I dropped my hands and opened my eyes.

There wasn't even a static charge at the end of my fingers.

Maybe it was because I was exerting too much effort. Or perhaps I wasn't putting in enough effort. Just maybe it was because I didn't realize the magnitude of the power Athena had bestowed upon me.

I frowned.

Well, that's not really a maybe.

I didn't understand the power.

I walked over to the side of the room and sat down to think.

Okay, it's not just the star power.

It's Astraea's star power.

Right. Okay. What did I know about her,

really? The goddess Astraea was known as the star maiden—but I don't even know if she was technically a goddess, really. If goddesses are a thing.

I caught myself and muttered aloud, "Which, apparently, they are. Let's not move backward, here, universe. Okay?"

She was the last of the immortals to live alongside humans during the Golden Age, one of man's five ages (according to the ancient Greeks). She abandoned the earth and humans due to humanity's wickedness, and legend has it she will return one day and bring with her another golden age.

So, that's the gist.

There was nothing in any myth I'd ever heard about her power being given to a witch. In fact, there wasn't much written about her ability at all. I'd read about her being careful and fair and about her being a leader. During her reign, the people she led shifted from conquering and fighting to caring for one another.

Until, you know, they didn't.

"Honor and love lay vanquished, Astraea, virgin divine, the last of the immortals, fled away," I murmured a line from the poem by Ovid to the empty room.

Ultimately meaningless, really. All of it was drivel when you—

Wait a minute.

For I was sent here in haste by the Virgin of the Stars Astraea herself, the nurse of law-abiding men; and what is more, law-loving Hermes has passed on this honor to me, that I alone by enforcing the laws of marriage may preserve the men whom I have sown.

Nonnus of Panopolis wrote that in…the *Dionysiaca*. I think he claimed…Aphrodite said it, maybe?

Ugh.

I ignored this stuff when Mom was homeschooling me.

Well, to be fair, it was the last of the epic poems, and my mother thought little of it—as a poem or as myth.

But my mother also said if things bubble up from the depths of your memory at certain times, pay attention because your subconscious could be trying to tell you something.

So there's that.

The nurse of the law-abiding men…

To be honest, I had no idea what that meant, but the line stuck in my head like a thorn. Even though I knew Astraea was regarded as a form of human justice, little information was available about what that entailed in practice. I just knew it was said that when she left, justice vanished from the earth.

Though in Shakespearean plays, Astraea was associated with the spirit of renewal.

I looked at my hands.

I knew Astraea amidst all the ancient Greeks' and Romans' history, poems, and claims. I knew what she was connected to. But I knew little about what she did or thought. The only action meticulously documented?

Astraea leaving for the stars.

Even though she was an important deity—Zeus did, after all, turn her into a constellation—her participation in the myths was limited. It's as if the stories were more interested in her essence than her actions. Who she was versus what she did.

Or...

I sat up.

Or the gods didn't want the answers written down, the keys explained, or the actions plotted for reference.

Could that be it?

Archie's words came back to me. *Look. I'm not Athena's only owl, and I haven't had a job in thousands of years.* Before that, he said, *You're a little extra. One of many little extras, by the way—you're not witch-Jesus, so don't get cocky.*

And the poem...*that I alone be enforcing the laws.*

That was *it.*

Astraea *had* returned.

But not in the way she had been.

The gods had ruled over the previous Golden Age as omnipotent super-powered royalty—and that age had failed. Another era followed in which mankind (and, to be honest, the paranormals) were doomed to a life of sickness and sorrow.

In short, the Greek gods ultimately failed to deliver on their promises. Instead, other gods and religions took their place as they faded into history and art—so much so most people don't believe they ever existed at all.

But they did.

* * *

"ARCHIE!" I shouted, jumping up to my feet.

The bird flew in through the high window, looking down. "Is everything all right?"

"So, bear with me. First, you said I'm not the only one with this power," I explained to the owl.

"So the magic isn't just one type of magic. I think it takes on the color of the person who has it and holds it. This is Astraea returning, as she promised, but it's more than that. The gods are attempting to resurrect a golden age, right? But what they were doing before wasn't working."

"Right," he said, looking at me with the wide eyes of a confused familiar. "I don't know that I would run and remind them that they failed. I'm just saying."

"No, you don't see? They are aware of their failure. They are, however, attempting once more, right? That's why I was given some power. Someone else has even more somewhere else. Actually," I said cocking my head, "there can be hundreds or thousands of people all over the world with a little bit of Astraea's justice power."

"Well, aren't you the designated revelator," Archie commented snarkily and stared at me in disbelief. "Man, we're well on our way to that golden age already with you as the prophet."

"Archie, I'm serious. Just think about it for a second. Possibilities, right? If they can give me Astraea's power, they can do the same for other people. The magic has now become a shared responsibility rather than a one person super-powered thing. It spreads it out everywhere. Puts justice magic in every corner of the world. Maybe those people are saving good people that shouldn't be killed all across the globe. Maybe they're doing something else with it. But it's like a satellite network spread out all over, bringing justice to every corner." I crossed my arms. "Honestly, it's kind of brilliant if you think about it."

I could hear the owl's feathers rustling. I looked up. Archie was flapping his wings and looking at me thoughtfully.

I clapped my hands together and pointed at him. "Ha. You're impressed. I can tell."

"It's quite possible," he said. "But you need to know something."

"What?" I said, sitting down.

I stared into his unblinking eyes. Archie's expression was suddenly serious, as if he wanted to communicate something urgent. He moved his head from side to side, looking over me from head to toe. Finally, with a deep breath, the owl hooted. Then he announced in a conspiratorial whisper, "You're not the only one with Astraea's magic."

I stared at him. "Are you kidding me?"

"I am not."

"I don't mean 'are you kidding me' as in are

you telling the truth. I mean 'are you kidding me' as in I already know that." I waited expectantly, but he didn't respond. Just stared down at me, looking pleased with himself for parroting my own theory back to me. "Archie, I literally *just* told you that."

The bird flapped his wings. "I know, but I feel like I need to be the one that comes up with these revelations to earn my keep."

"But you didn't."

"But I could have."

"But you didn't."

"You know, I never thought I'd say this, but maybe the gods are on to something with this 'shared responsibility' thing." Archie cocked his head, changing gears immediately and growing serious.

"You think?"

"I mean, what's the worst they can do if they— or we—fail? No one has tried it this way, you know. Sharing power." Archie shook his tail feathers and jumped down from the beam onto my shoulder. "If they fail, though, the risk is that they'll maybe think it's not worth it to try." I looked up into his eyes. "That would be a dark day. The day they stop trying."

"That would be a dark day," I agreed, even though I wasn't sure that it would be.

"On the other hand," he said, "you know what would be another dark day? The day the gods defied their roles, broke the rules, and came back to rule themselves." Archie shuddered. "You met Dionysus. Would you want that dude in charge of anything? I mean, for real. Have you ever seen Jabuticaba grapes? It's like the platypus of grapes. Seriously." Archie rubbed his head against my temple. "Good job coming up with this."

"Thanks. It was some of the things that you said that made me realize," I told him. "So, you don't have to fake coming up with a revelation."

The owl looked proudly at me. "Really?"

I nodded. "Really."

Archie looked away and shrugged as if he didn't care, but I could tell he was touched that anything he said led to my revelation. "Maybe people could really change," he said quietly. "Wouldn't that be something? People could actually become better. Society could be better." He let out a purring sound. "It would be nice to be a part of something like that. Even if just a small part."

I nodded.

The owl looked the room over. "Back to the

subject at hand, I guess. You know what happened with the panther?"

I bit my lip. "Um. Yeah, no. I didn't get to that."

Archie rolled his eyes.

"Okay, okay, I got it."

I placed my hand on the wall, Archie firmly on my shoulder.

* * *

I COULD SEE the memories of the room in my mind's eye now—as if understanding Astraea's power had cleared the fog keeping me from other truths. Thousands of years of memories were strewn across the wall—even though this building couldn't be over fifty years old.

The atmosphere was thick with the weight of a thousand past lives that had shaped the room's walls, floor, furnishings, and even the ceiling, chair, and table. Each tale gave the impression that another hand had scratched into the wall's history, another protective layer to guard the memories it contained.

"Whoa," I murmured.

I saw the panther in the room, but the cat was never with Alexarchos.

Then I could see Alexarchos—always with his eyes closed and always alone.

Then I saw the panther sleeping, but Alexarchos was nowhere to be found.

Neither of them was ever in the same room as anyone else.

"Can you see anything?" Archie asks.

"Yes, but nothing that tells me what happened to the panther," I answer.

I was looking for something in the room to help me, but I could find nothing. It was just a constant coin flip—Alexarchos, then the panther, then Alexarchos, then the panther again. I didn't know what to do next.

I was frustrated and pushed deeper into the vision.

The panther comes back into view, but... something was different.

It's more than just a physical being; its spirit clings to it like a haze. It has deep, vibrant fur and a thick, black tail. Its eyes are two radiant pools of blue that seem to glow from within, like twin fires burning within the wood. I'm enveloped by the scent of blue roses. It's a familiar fragrance somehow, and yet I can't remember when I've smelled it before. It's light and sweet, like a spring breeze.

Its enormous head, black as tar, was sharply turned. Under its great eyes, I could almost detect a smile. And it's…

…looking at me. At least it seems to be.

What the—

"Hello to you both," she says. Her voice is breathy and laced with laughter. "I've been wondering how long it would take you to give this a whirl." She is beautiful, with bright blue eyes that seem to know everything. The panther's oddly colored gaze locks directly into mine. "It's nice to meet you."

But she *can't* see me.

She's a *memory*.

Memories can't talk.

"Hello?" she says again, slightly more impatient.

"Are you talking to me?" I ask, even though I felt ridiculous doing it.

This is a vision. Nothing more.

Though admittedly, this vision feels so real I want to touch the panther to see if it will go away or become more solid somehow.

"I am."

"Are you Pantera?"

"I am."

Huh.

Okay.

Unexpected.

"Can you tell me what happened to you?" I ask her. Deep within my mind, I *know* that I shouldn't be able to converse with a memory. My power is a simple one, an observational one—I can see only what other people or things have seen. The power to communicate over long distances is incredibly rare. It almost always required a fancy cauldron and tons of spells.

And yet...I know, somehow, this panther is no memory.

It feels too real.

"Why?" the cat asks.

"I hate dealing with cats," Archie muttered. "So unhelpful."

Archie, still riding on my shoulder, could see the panther, too.

"I'm trying to help Alexarchos."

Pantera's eyes flicker. "Alexarchos. He's in no danger." She cocks her head. "Neither am I." Then she shakes her head. "The only person that was really in danger was you, and that danger has passed now."

I stare blankly. Was the Apollo card somehow about me? "What?"

The big cat flew through the air and landed

right in front of me, staring me down with those bright blue eyes. "I would like nothing more than to help you," she purrs. "I would love to tell you everything I know. But I can't do that."

"Why not?"

Her tail lashes about behind her. "It's complicated."

"What's complicated?"

"Everything."

"Okay. Fine. No problem. Can you at least tell me what you remember?"

A colossal paw—almost as big as my head— swiped toward me playfully, and Pantera shook her head. "It's not my story to tell."

"You're as useless as a screen door on a submarine," Archie muttered at the cat.

I stifled a laugh, but just barely. "Okay, Pantera, then what's your story to tell?" I asked, hoping to find a simple, open-ended question for the panther that would get me some kind of helpful information.

"Oddly enough, that's not my story to tell, either." She rolls over, turning her back toward me. "If you want to know what happened to me, you're going to have to talk to the next person who remembers me."

"If you gave this cat a penny for her thoughts,

I think you'd get change," Archie told me, his tone frustrated. "What does that even mean?"

I was beginning to agree with Archie and wondered if this blue-eyed panther was distantly related to a sphinx. "My owl has a point, Pantera. What do you mean?"

"I want to. Truly. I do want to help you." The big cat rolls on her back and looks up at me. "But I'm not allowed." Pantera yawned, showing off a gaping mouth full of dangerously sharp teeth.

"Why not?" I ask her. "Who said you're not allowed?"

"It would break the rules."

I shake my head. "What rules? I haven't been given any rules."

"The ones I'm not allowed to talk about." I couldn't help but notice her razor-sharp claws as she rolled onto her back.

I wasn't too concerned because this was technically a vision, but I wasn't wholly unconcerned either. I'd never communicated with my visions, and my visions had never spoken with me. Until I knew more, I would assume that vision and voice might just vibrate at the same frequency as panther claws.

"You really don't listen, do you? It's not my story to tell. Maybe you should go talk to the next person who remembers me," she says. "Use your power if you don't figure it out beforehand. Look for me in their memories."

"But—"

She sighs. "I don't know what else to tell you, and you're beginning to make me cross. I don't wish to ruin your Christmas, but I will do so if you continue to ruin my nap."

"Cats," Archie said with disgust.

"Fine," I told the panther. "We'll go. You're sure you're not in danger?"

"Get out," she responded coldly. "You started off this conversation with that assurance from me. I'm not going in a circle with you." She then gives me an almost impish grin. "Good luck."

When I try to focus on the panther again, it seems to blur and fade out.

Finally, I couldn't see her anymore, and the vision was gone.

I take a deep breath. "Archie?"

He stares at me. "Yeah?"

"This god stuff?"

"Yeah?"

"Super annoying."

"Tell me about it," Archie agreed. "I think they're the reason Santa even *has* a naughty list."

CHAPTER SIXTEEN

"*Y*ou're going to have to talk to the next person who remembers me," I said, finally, to the assembled group. "That's what the vision said. Or what the panther in the vision said."

"I don't understand what that means at all." Eddie frowned down at the table. "Is it some kind of cryptic clue we have to figure out? A word puzzle of some kind?"

I could see Dionysus and Ariadne approaching us, their solemn-looking butler trailing behind with a tray of fancy-looking drinks. "If we don't want those two to overhear," I said, gesturing toward the gods, "we may want to figure it out fast. Unless it's one of them." I tapped my finger on the picnic table outside the stable. "I mean, technically, they remember the panther, right? The three of them." I looked at Archie. "Do we just wait for one of them to recall something and then question them?"

"It could be that simple," the owl responded, still tucked into my shoulder. "It's also possible that eliciting information from a cat is a futile exercise."

I raised my eyebrow. "You don't think that was a clue, then?"

"I think the problem with cats is that they look at a moth or a serial killer with a knife with the same expression," Archie retorted. "Her remark could have been a sign directing us to the right place. On the other hand, her comment could also be indicative of a big cat who just wants us to leave so she can nap."

"What do you think the 'visions talk back' thing was, anyway?" Emma asked me as Dionysus and Ariadne stepped up to the table. "That's never happened to you before, has it?" I shook my head. "I can still hear Archie talking, so I don't know if the cat's claim that no one's in danger anymore is entirely accurate."

Archie hopped off my shoulder and onto the table. "The star card technically didn't drop, and we never really figured out what the Apollo card meant, specifically. Not with any certainty. We guessed. Well, you guessed. And," the owl said, pacing, "Ami's not really explaining much. Speaking of, did you get a hold of her while we were in there chatting with the panther?"

Emma winced as she looked at the owl with a pained expression. "Why's he screeching at me? Did I make him mad or something?"

"I'm not screeching at you." Archie stopped pacing and stared at Emma. "I haven't raised my voice to you all day. Well, not that I remember, anyway."

Emma looked at me. "Why's he hooting like that?"

"He's not." I looked back at her, surprised. "You can't understand him?" Then, without waiting for her to answer, I turned to Eddie. "What about you? Did you understand what he just said?"

Eddie nodded. "He asked Emma if she called your sister."

"No, he didn't." Emma looked slightly alarmed. "He just hooted and hissed. He didn't talk to me." Her face fell. "Are you serious? After all this, am I back to being the odd one out again?" She slammed back in her seat sullenly. "I swear, a woman could get a complex from this, you know."

I gave her a sympathetic half-smile. "Let's try and figure out when this happened. What's the last thing you heard him say?"

Emma thought a second. "That Pantera might not want to get involved."

"Why would Emma suddenly stop understanding me?" Archie mumbled under his breath. "Did something change?" He turned his head quickly and raised his voice. "What changed? Nothing changed while we were sitting here. Or something did change, but we don't know it changed. Is it over?" Suddenly, his demeanor brightened. "Hey. Can I go get my evening snack now?"

"No, you're wrong." Detective Renzo said, leaning back in his chair.

"I beg your pardon, bozo?" Archie glared. The bird bowed his head shamefully, cleared his throat, and looked Renzo in the eye. "Sorry. *Detective* Bozo."

"Something did change." Renzo brushed aside the owl's offense and cast a glance my way. "Archie jumped off your shoulder and onto the table. Everything he said after he was on the table, Emma didn't seem to understand. She heard it as screeching and hissing."

I went back over the events since I sat down in my mind. Eddie Renzo was right.

Not only did Emma stop understanding Archie once he jumped off my shoulder, but it also hit me like a thunderbolt that Archie'd been perched on my shoulder the second time I tried to use Astraea's power. *Not* the first time. And the *second* time opened up a channel to Pantera, allowing me to communicate with the big cat's spirit.

Was that the determining factor in mastering the "gift?"

Maybe Archie was not simply a divine messenger and guide. Perhaps our bond was critical to maximizing the star power's potential.

It would certainly explain why *he* was in trouble, too.

If I was correct, he was probably in far less trouble for his salty mouth than for his constant disappearance. Even when he was present for cases, he usually observed what was going on from a distance.

I looked up at Ariadne, who stood silent beside her husband. "Do you know anything about any of this?"

"I'm the goddess of paths," she responded. I noticed she didn't ask for clarification regarding what I meant by "any of this." Her tone wasn't unkind, but it wasn't helpful, either. I already knew she wasn't going to give me an answer. "I can guide your feet onto the path you were meant to take, but you must take it."

Eddie sighed.

"What's wrong?" Archie hopped back up on my shoulder.

"The deeper we get into this, the more I realize it has nothing to do with the parties that are taking place," Renzo said with a brief smile. "I also can't very well arrest Dionysus for them—even though I should." He glanced at the god. "I don't suppose you'll make a full confession that you and your priests have been throwing parties in people's homes, stealing their valuables, and then promise never to do it again, would you?"

Ariadne reached out to silence Dionysus as he opened his mouth to speak. "Your assistance has been greatly appreciated, wolf. The paths of those learning lessons from the parties will come to an end." Her eyes burned with determination. "Those that have not found their paths will be led to them in…other ways. Ways that do not conflict with your chosen path."

We stared at each other for a brief moment, saying nothing.

"There's a story there," Archie said.

"Hey—I can understand him again," Emma said with surprise.

"There's our answer, then," Eddie said, nodding. "Emma can understand the owl if he's in contact with you." For a long moment, the detective was lost in thought. "I wonder if this is something that's always been the case or something that changed because the two of you were drifting apart."

"Two of who?" Archie asked.

"You and Astra. I mean, it's obvious that's why all this was done."

"Oh, it's obvious, is it, you ninnyhammer?" Archie glared at him. "We both met you, what, this morning? So now you're an expert, are you?"

Renzo met the bird's angry stare and said nothing.

"Thank you for controlling your sour-tongued self," I told Archie sarcastically.

"You're welcome," he responded proudly. "Thank you for recognizing my effort."

Emma interrupted Archie's unwarranted victory lap. "So, getting back to the question—it's new. I've only been able to understand Archie during cases. But it didn't matter whether he was in contact with Astra or not."

Archie and I exchanged glances. Our eyes locked as we both seemed to recognize that Renzo actually had a point. We hadn't been performing as well as either of us had presumed. "You know, at least they like us well enough to plan this whole conspiracy just to get us back on the right track," I told him quietly.

"True." He looked at Dionysus. "Hey, Drunky McBoozehead. We're on the right track. Well done. Do we still have to find your stupid panther?"

We all jumped back as Dionysus lunged for the owl.

* * *

WE SAT OUTSIDE in the backyard and discussed what to do next in hushed tones.

After talking to Ami, Emma felt like we should travel back to Forkbridge and talk to Alexarchos again. Emma pointed out that we had a far different understanding of the situation now than we did when we talked to him earlier this morning. So she thought going back to the beginning was a good idea.

On the other hand, Eddie wanted to go back down to the beach to try and pick up the panther's scent again.

My phone buzzed. It was Ami.

HEY. IT'S GETTING LATE. HAVEN'T HEARD FROM YOU.

I laughed and replied with a text explaining that I had had no reason to text her since she informed me she would not help me.

DON'T GET SASSY, SIS. ALEXARCHOS SAYS THAT YOU TWO SHOULD TALK. HE JUST REMEMBERED SOMETHING ABOUT THE PANTHER.

I stared at the text. "Oh, come on," I muttered.

Emma looked concerned. "What's wrong?"

"You're going to have to talk to the next person who remembers me," I repeated to the table. "That's what the vision said, right? Well, guess what text Ami just sent me?" I read it word for word and looked up. "Do you ever get the feeling that you're being manipulated by forces beyond your understanding?"

"I don't, no," Emma responded cheerfully. "But do I ever get the feeling that *you're* being manipulated by forces beyond your understanding?" She tossed her hair out of her eyes. "All the damn time, Astra. In fact, so much so I'm surprised you said that to me without a trace of irony."

Our group fell into a brief, thoughtful silence.

Then, without warning, Eddie broke it.

"Okay, who's driving?" Eddie, shoving his chair back and springing to his feet, wondered aloud. "Come on, if we're heading to Forkbridge, we have to get moving. It's already getting late." He looked at his phone. "It's past seven. If we leave at this very moment and we speed, we can get there at around ten."

Emma raised her head, attempting to conceal her excitement at the prospect of racing back to Forkbridge while violating speed limits—but her expression wouldn't be out of place on a giddy schoolgirl. "I'll drive."

I stood up, Archie still on my shoulder, and handed my phone to Birch. "Here," I said, unlocking it, and then asked him to input his phone number.

He nodded and began tapping.

"We'll contact you as soon as we have any information," I informed the Greek gods, reinforcing that they were not invited on the road trip.

"Of course," Ariadne answered, her eyes guarded. "We have a Christmas party to attend, anyway—but Montgomery will be available if you have any questions."

I left Palm Beach wondering who hosted Olympians' Christmas parties.

* * *

I SAT in the back seat with the owl, discussing how our relationship had devolved into a series of minor missteps that had landed us in hot water. Archie initially looked up at me nervously, but as we discussed what had brought us here, he looked more and more embarrassed.

"Look, no one gave me a handbook on how to do this, so I didn't know," he insisted. "It makes sense, though. I wasn't high up on the list of divine owls, you know." The bird, strapped into the backseat of Emma's car, looked glum as he apologized again. "I just want you to know that if I had known, I would have done better." He glowered fiercely. "My boss was an idiot."

"Wasn't your boss Athena?" Emma called from the front seat, her eyes glued to the road as she wove in and out of traffic.

"Well, ultimately. She's, like, the CEO, I guess. We have middle management. My boss was a dragon that liked brandy just a little bit too much.

I should have known he was drunk when he thought Florida was in Macedonia."

"A dragon," Emma said, her tone stunned.

"Yep."

"There are dragons…"

"Yep."

I shoved my bag down into the footwell to give Archie a bit more room. "I think you and I both made some mistakes, Archimedes," I told him, scratching him on the head. "I had little experience with animals because my mother never allowed us to have pets, and I never studied anything about familiars at the Ministry because the military didn't have any."

"That was probably part of the problem with you people, you know," Archie told me, his expression judgmental.

I couldn't figure out why my feelings about everything seemed to shift so dramatically in a single day. I was less irritated with Archie and more sympathetic to him. Yes, having gods intervene in your life to try to teach you lessons would almost certainly result in some kind of attitude adjustment—but I didn't feel regretful for my mistakes so much as reinvigorated.

It was weird to me how easily I accepted what happened.

How instantly everything changed for me.

"Familiars aren't really animals," Eddie said from the passenger side. Despite being a tough cop and a werewolf, he gripped the edge of the seat tightly and stared straight ahead, his expression nervous as Emma zipped through traffic. "Most sacred animals aren't reflective so much of the animal itself but the god it represents. So I'd think of Archie less like an owl and more like the embodiment of some of Athena's qualities."

"What qualities, do you think?" I asked, curious.

"Well, from what I've seen?" Eddie glanced back at me. "And before I say anything, let's remember Archie is right—I've known you both for a day. But Athena's first quality, her *original* one, was as a protectress. She's also got a dual-nature, really—sometimes she's really masculine, and sometimes she's really feminine." He turned back. "Seems like you embody some of those qualities, too."

"Athena is super awkward with sex and romance, too, you know," Emma said gleefully. "Talk about embodying—"

"Hey! I thought this was about Archie?" I snapped.

"I don't know what Emma's talking about. But, I promise you, I am not awkward with the ladies at all," Archie bragged.

"What ladies?" Emma asked.

"There are ladies," Archie told her. "Oh, believe you me, Sullivan. There are ladies. *Lots* of ladies."

"I thought owls mate for life?"

"Not this owl," Archie told Emma.

"In other words, you have commitment issues?" Eddie joked.

"You know, instead of talking about *my* love life, maybe we should be talking about Alexarchos, the panther, and what we think is going to happen when—"

I sat upright. "Wait a minute. Say that again?"

"Stop talking about my love life!" Archie hooted.

"No, not that. You said 'Alexarchos the panther' like Alexarchos was the panther," I said briskly, leaning forward. The hair on the back of my neck had stood up at Archie's words, and my mind raced through the things I'd seen.

"No, I did not," the owl said, looking at me oddly. "I said *Alexarchos, the panther.* There was a comma between them. So Alexarchos isn't a panther."

But…but…was he?

"Eddie?" I asked, leaning forward. "When you were trying to get the panther's scent from the stable she lived in, how did you know which was her scent and which was Alexarchos' scent? Like, when I asked you to follow the panther's scent, how did you know you were following her scent?"

"There was only one scent in the stable," Eddie responded, turning to face me, his expression both surprised and questioning. "I mean, I could tell other people had been in the stable at some point. Many people. But there was only one scent that had really permeated the building, and that was the one I followed."

"If two people lived in the building, both their scents would be detectable, though? Like, they'd be equally strong, equally detectable?"

"Should be," he answered, nodding. Then he frowned. "So, wait—you're sure Alexarchos *lived* there?"

"He said he did. That he was sleeping, and when he woke up, the panther was gone," I said, my voice rising with excitement. "And it's not just that. I saw it in the vision when I went back the second time. I saw the panther, I saw him—but never, not once, did I ever see them in the building simultaneously. Never together."

"Alexarchos is a shifter?" Emma asked, surprised.

"Alexarchos is a liar," Archie spat from the backseat. "A big honking liar."

"What did he say?" Emma asked, glancing toward Archie in the rearview mirror. I looked over and realized I was no longer in contact with him.

"Oh, sorry." I reached back and slipped my hand underneath Archie's talon. He gripped it and repeated his pronouncement. "The story he told us was...damn, did he lie about everything he said?" I looked back at Archie. "That picture in Apollo's house. They knew each other." I slammed back against the back seat. "Are you serious? Was this whole thing just a gigantic, steaming pile of—"

"Now, wait a minute," Emma said, cutting me off.

"For what? This is ridiculous."

"Look, I get how you feel—I went through this with Rex and his complete and utter manipulation of my life until the two of us worked things out, right?" Emma glanced briefly into the backseat.

"But I need to point out he did that because I *probably* wouldn't just listen to what he had to say. I mean, yeah, okay, he never tried. But if I'm honest, I probably wouldn't have listened to him."

"Okay," I said, not understanding.

"So, I have to ask you—would you have listened to anyone?" she asked. "Because if you really think about it, I think you have to admit you probably wouldn't have. Yesterday, you wouldn't even grant these gods the possibility of existence. Archie wasn't really helping—"

"Hey!" he snapped.

"Well, were you? Were you doing anything other than demanding Astra believe or making fun of her for not believing?"

"No, but there's no need to point it out like that! We're over it!"

"All I'm saying is you needed a wake-up call," Emma said, her voice sober and shooting me a serious look through the rearview mirror. "Both of you. Look, things happen to people all the time. Situations that change them. Things they see that change their perspective. Who's to say that those occurrences aren't the result of divine providence? Holy interference? Heavenly post-it-notes? Angelic two-by-fours?"

"Okay, okay, I hear you," I said, muttering as I looked out the window.

"Do you?" she said.

"I said I hear you," I told her sharply.

"Astra, don't look at this all as a manipulation," Eddie said quietly. Emma nodded. "Look at it as a gift."

"Right. A gift! Perfect. Merry Christmas!" Emma called exuberantly.

"Hey, Speed Racer, we probably solved the case," Archie snapped at Emma before I could respond. "You wanna slow down before we're all stains on the pavement?"

Emma didn't slow down.

"Emma!" the owl shouted as Emma's speed demon sleeper flew through the darkness. "No need for speed!"

"The gods obviously want us back in Forkbridge," she answered thoughtfully. The needle on the speedometer leaped forward, and Emma's lead foot slammed against the gas pedal. "May as well take advantage of the hand of divine protection."

CHAPTER SEVENTEEN

*W*e made it back to the house by half past nine.

Yes, a three and a half hour drive took us just two and a half hours.

I wish I could credit magic or some divine intervention, but it was Emma's lead foot that kept us racing toward my destiny and a hair's breadth from killing ourselves along the highway. I'd be surprised if her tires still had rubber.

"Who's that?" Detective Renzo asked as we pulled up in front of Arden House.

Alexarchos stood on the front porch, leaning heavily on the columned entrance. He rolled his shoulders back, cocking his head to one side as he watched our approach. The muscles in his face were locked in a carefully neutral expression

"That," I told Eddie, "is either one of Dionysus's priests in charge of watching his panther, the actual panther shifter themself, or some third option we haven't even figured out yet. Heck, maybe he's Santa Claus—weirder things have happened." I opened the door and got out of the car, Archie on my shoulder. "What he is for sure is the dude that started today's little adventure."

"Interesting fashion sense for Florida," Renzo responded. He opened the passenger door of Emma's Malibu and stepped onto the dirt driveway in front of Arden House. "Do I need to know pronouns or something?"

"Welcome back," Alexarchos called across the lawn before I could answer the pronoun question. "How was Palm Beach?"

"Rich and overly greedy," Emma said as we walked toward him. "You ever wear anything other than black?"

"My dear," he responded, his impish grin reminding me a little of Apollo, "I'm a priest of Dionysus. I'm supposed to be somber."

"I would not have guessed that at all," Eddie

said, looking the priest up and down. "Somber isn't a word I would have associated with that guy at all. He looks like he'd grin at a funeral."

"You wound me," Alexarchos said with a mocking fondness. He looked down at Eddie. "It also depends on whose funeral." The priest winked. "I know these two lovely ladies, but you, handsome, I'm unfamiliar with." Alexarchos' eyebrows shot up. "Have we met?"

"No," Eddie said, "but I've seen you around Palm Beach every once in a while. I'm Detective Eddie Renzo with the Palm Beach Police Department."

"Ah," Alexarchos said, "so you're the one causing so much trouble for my friends." Eddie raised an eyebrow. "The ones that have been throwing the parties."

Eddie tensed.

"Relax, Detective. I understand my mistress has assured you those vulgarities will come to an end in your jurisdiction."

"And how would you know that? You've been here all day."

Alexarchos looked at me, his gaze steady. "Hello, again, Astra."

"Yeah, hi, and I thought you were hiding here

because you were afraid Dionysus was going to execute you for losing his panther. Or allowing it to be stolen." I crossed my arms. "Or, you know, whatever story you concocted this morning. I'm not sure what you lied about at this point. But I know you lied."

The punk's face was adorned with a broad, endearing smile. "I'd heard you were smart. Both of you," he said, gesturing toward Emma. "I really appreciated the opportunity to see how convincing I could be." He looked proud. "I did get you to Palm Beach. That was my first mission."

"And your second?" I snapped, irritated.

Alexarchos laughed and threw his head back. He pushed himself off the column and stepped back. He carried himself like a legend's hero, a fable's prince, a man poised to meet his fate. His shoulders were erect, and his head was held high. His body seemed to exude a steady stream of confidence. "It is getting late, I agree." Turning to Emma and Eddie, he bowed his head. "If you two will be so kind as to give Astra and me a few moments?"

Emma frowned. "You want us to leave?" She glanced over at me, a concerned look on her face. "I don't know that I'm comfortable with that. Not to mention the fact that I won't sleep all night wondering how this all ended."

"No, no, I wouldn't dream of it." He glanced toward the front door. "*Your* journey ends right behind that door. But, I promise you, once you enter, you'll have all the answers you need." Alexarchos turned. "Astra and I have a few more things to discuss."

Emma and Eddie didn't move.

The priest's eyes flickered, and his mouth tightened slightly. He didn't look like a man used to being ignored. Finally, he cleared his throat and aimed a bright smile at Emma. "I can tell you're unsure. Is there anything I can say to help this process along?" Alexarchos asked.

"Look, I don't want to leave her alone with you. Not until we know what you are, what this is, and what you're doing. For sure."

"Well, I know what he is," Eddie told her, his eyes steady and level on the leather-clad man. The werewolf's posture was wary and alert. "I can sense the predator in him. He's a panther shifter. You know, what we talked about in the car?" Eddie nodded sharply once. "You were right, Astra."

"You get used to it," Emma told him.

"Well, one does call out to another, yes? In any

case, you know I won't change standing on someone's front porch in full view of the street." Alexarchos turned and gestured with a jerk of his head to the door. "Please. Go into the house, where everything will be made clear. Astra and I must speak alone."

Emma and Eddie studied him for another moment. Then, finally, Emma turned to me. "This is your rodeo, Astra. Do you want us to stay with you or go inside?"

I realized I *should* be feeling on alert.

Alexarchos had clearly lied to me, there were gods involved, and my family was acting weird. I should check on my family first. I should want Emma and Eddie with me just in case things went sideways. Nothing about the events of the day told me I should trust this man and his complete change of personality, total shift of story.

But I wasn't feeling on alert. My gut said he was right.

We needed to talk.

I looked at Archie.

"Yeah, I agree," he said with a nod. "No idea why, but yeah."

"I'll be fine," I assured Emma. "Go into the house. I'll be in there in a minute." I gestured toward the door, and Emma stared at me for a moment. Then she nodded.

"Slightly more than a minute," Alexarchos said as the two moved toward the entrance. "But I promise you, Astra is safe with me."

"If anything happens...." Eddie said, looking from me to the priest. "Anything at all."

"I'll be fine," I insisted, feeling a little irritated again.

They climbed the stairs. The front door swung inward toward the hallway, and for a moment, Emma's face was bathed in soft golden light. She took a final look over her shoulder, a slow nod of her head. Eddie closed the door behind them.

"Well," I said. "It looks like we're alone. What do you want to talk about?" I asked. He didn't answer. We just stood in front of the columns for a few long moments, watching each other.

Finally, Alexarchos strode across the porch and sat down on the front steps. He patted the step next to him. "Come," he said. "Let's talk about what happens next."

* * *

"I DON'T WANT to talk about what happens next," I told him as I sat down next to him. "I want to talk about what already happened. And why. Why you lied to me."

"I lied to you?" Alexarchos crossed his arms. "You really think so?"

"Alexarchos, I'm not going to play games with you," I said. "What you said this morning about the panther, you running from Dionysus, all of it. It wasn't true."

"You really think so?" Alexarchos face was a picture of innocence. His ice-blue eyes sparkled mischievously in the darkness.

I looked at Archie. "Can you see why I wanted to avoid the Olympians like the plague now?"

Archie snorted. "Um, wait a minute. You didn't want to *avoid* the Olympians. You didn't believe the plague existed. You know what happens to people who don't believe a rampant plague exists?" the owl asked, one feather-eyebrow raised. "They get the plague!"

"Your owl is wise," Alexarchos said.

"You're the panther, dude," I said, ignoring their observations. "Your panther can't be stolen. It's you. You're her. Why did you even show up here? Who put you up to this? And why did you lie to me, forcing me to shlep all over Florida, fearing for the safety of my family?"

"I am you, too," Alexarchos said, his trickster tone settling into a confessional one.

"What the hell does that even mean?"

"I was like you once. Well, the way you were yesterday," he admitted, his expression slightly embarrassed. "I didn't want to be a shifter. Didn't think I was one, actually." He leaned forward and looked me in the eye. "I don't know why I was abandoned as a baby. Maybe my parents were killed by the Witches' Council, maybe they were arrested. But I was found in a motel room, abandoned. The humans put me with a human family, and I don't mind telling you that's not a great place for a shifter to grow up."

"I'm sorry," I told him sincerely.

He nodded. "I thought I was crazy, having this voice in my head talking to me. You'd think having a cat talking to you in your head would be cool, right?" He looked at me and smiled a gentle smile. "But when no one around you knows why you have a fully formed being inside you talking to you? They thought I was crazy. And me?" His smile faded. "I didn't know what to think."

"I'm so sorry that happened to you, but I don't see how this has anything to do with me at all," I said, shifting to face him. "I wasn't abandoned. I was raised in a coven family. I've always known I was a witch."

"You're right; we're not exactly the same. No two people on the planet are exactly the same," he admitted. "But not only did I not know what I was, even once I had a clue what the answer could be? I denied it. Actively. I rejected it as hard as I could. For quite a while." Alexarchos thrust his arm out and rolled up his sleeve. There, amid the tattooed images of animals and skeletons, were three words.

BANISH THIS DARKNESS

"Dionysus found me at a party," he told me, smiling at the memory. "He touched the words and asked me if the spell I had written on my skin had managed to silence the panther that lived within me just waiting to live. To breathe." His eyes teared up. "For me, it was instantaneous like a thunderbolt. Another being acknowledging who I was, what I was? It was...was like a taste of Ganymede's ambrosia. The awareness was a thunderbolt. The acceptance?" He smiled. "That was everything."

"That's why you became an Orphic priest."

Alexarchos nodded. "Dionysus was the first person to see me for who I was. And yes, I realize the gods have their challenges," he said with a chuckle. "My life unfolded from that moment. I stopped fighting who I was and who I was born to be. I wanted to take risks, be creative, to do something special with my life."

"Congratulations."

He smiled again. "My bond with Pantera means more to me now than I ever could have imagined as a sullen, depressed fifteen-year-old kid unsure of my place in the world." He looked me in the eye. "You needed to do so as well. Stop fighting what you are. You have to take control of your own life, Astra—or else someone else will."

"Wait a minute. We're not the same. I've never even seen Athena," I told him. "I've never had faith in anything but myself—"

"That is untrue," Alexarchos said, cutting me off. "You had faith in the military until it betrayed you. You have faith in Emma and her friendship. Ami and her sight. Althea and her potions. Ayla and her—" Alexarchos paused. "Well, Ayla is young yet. She'll find her stability." We both laughed. "Your mother, despite your difficulties, believes in you and you her. Your aunt? You have no greater champion than your Aunt Gwennie."

"Okay, yeah, I struggle with my faith in others," I admitted.

"And working with the gods would help you with that. We are not in ancient times," he pointed out, raising an eyebrow. "What they expect from us and what we are willing to give as signs of faith is no longer set in stone. They have grown. *We* have grown. Faith in Athena is not an absolute, Astra," he explained, nodding. "It's a negotiation. With desires and gifts of honor on *both* sides. It's a relationship."

"But to negotiate? To have a relationship? To negotiate a relationship? You have to believe the person you're negotiating with exists," Archie, who had been quiet, suddenly spoke up. "There's only so much even a god would want to try if you keep insulting them."

Alexarchos nodded. "Well said, Archimedes."

"Yeah, I know," Archie responded.

I rolled my eyes. "So all this was just to get me to believe?"

"I was telling you the truth," he said. "Athena did refuse to come to Dionysus's party. And she did threaten to steal Pantera and me. But Ariadne believed her frustration—her dark mood—was partly born from your rejection of her gift and your continued rejection of her. Well," Alexarchos said, pointing to my owl, "that and Archie's lack of—"

"We all know what Archie lacked!" the owl snapped. "Let's move on!"

"That exchange formed the seed of a plan to help you, help him, and help her. It is Apollo and Ariadne's holiday gift to Athena. And also, of course, their gift to you." The Orphic priest smiled. "Many demand proof before extending belief. You got it without asking. You should feel honored that your faith was so important to them."

Alexarchos talked like a priest, and what he was saying was somewhat hard to follow. The core of his message, though, was clear. "Hey, I said I believe they exist now. Good job. Well done. If that was your goal, you hit it right on the mark. But I didn't say I had faith in them. Let's not get carried away here."

Alexarchos laughed a rich, deep laugh.

"So, it's over then?" Archie asked him. "This whole 'find the missing panther that's not missing' shtick?"

"Not quite." Alexarchos stood up and reached out his hand. "You saw the past through Ariadne's eyes. The present through Apollo's. Through that door," Alexarchos nodded toward my mother's front door, "I invite you to see the future through your own eyes. The final answer to what you need? It's in there."

After hearing his words, I felt as if a heavy weight had been lifted from my shoulders. I felt whole, as if something had been missing and had now been restored. It was as if a massive wall had just collapsed.

"Let's do it," I said, stepping up on the porch.

I reached out and opened the door.

CHAPTER EIGHTEEN

a party.

It's a Christmas party.

"This is my future?" I whispered to Archie.

The party was in full swing by the time I arrived. Once I walked in, I was hit with a wave of sound—music, laughter, and conversation. Christmas decorations were everywhere as if they'd been there all season, filling the space with color and light. There were Christmas trees in every room, lights, wreaths hanging from the ceiling, and an enormous fireplace blazing in the living room. The whole place smelled like gingerbread.

"I don't get it," the owl admitted. "Are we in an alternate timeline?"

The place was packed with people I knew and many I didn't. Some of them were in roaring good moods, drinking, eating, and dancing. Others were sitting on the couches, talking in small clusters. The living room opened onto the dining room, which was full of long tables covered in white tablecloths. Elves—real ones, not the Christmas idea of them—refilled plates of hors d'oeuvres like someone had called a paranormal catering company.

"Alexarchos," I said, turning back toward the hallway. "What is this?"

"He said the final answer to what you need was in here," Ami said as she rushed up and embraced me, her head on the opposite shoulder from Archie. "So, what you need is in here! Actually, a *lot* of what you need is in here. You should see the holiday cookies. And there's like three different kinds of cheesecake."

"Can *you* tell me why this is here? Who are these people?" I asked Ami.

"These are people in your life, Astra. Your past, your present, your future. And they're all here because you need to be here," Ami said. "The gods wanted to make sure you knew this is where you belong. This is where you're meant to be."

Nodding to Ami, Alexarchos walked over to

Apollo and shook his head. Then, in an affectionate embrace, they held hands and smiled at each other.

"That's it?" I asked her, confused.

"Where you truly belong isn't a simple thing, sis."

I spotted the Palm Beach gods across the room and watched Dionysus and Ariadne laugh at something my mother said. "How on earth did you guys throw a Christmas party together in a day? And how did they"—I pointed at the wine god and his wife—"get from Palm Beach to here faster than we did?"

"Divine intervention helps explain everything you're asking me," Ami told me with a wink. "They wanted to be here at the end."

"Okay, bird guide, help me understand," I said to Archie, confused. "What does it all mean?"

"Well, I'm not the expert—"

"Only you are, technically, the expert."

He glared at me. "—but I think you keep doing what you're doing," Archie said with a shrug. "You're fulfilling your purpose, and your purpose is to help people, to make a difference. And I'm sure you'll figure out how and where and who and what and all that—but I think this is a message that you're not alone. That this is where you should be." Archie craned his neck as he took count of the crowded room. "We all learn and grow and change as we go along. And we all help each other along the way." He extended his wing toward the crowded room. "Your help."

"Huh." My eyes scanned my family, friends— the mayor of Cassandra, the captain. My aunt talking to Rex, Emma's vampire brother. "Is that how you understand this?" I asked, still looking around the room.

"I guess so," Archie said. "I mean, that's my role in this, right? I help you figure things out, see what you need to see, remind you of who you are when you're lost—"

"That only works when you're not lost, too, you know," I murmured. "Speaking of, are you going to stay a pocket-sized owl now?"

"Oh, I'm so glad you said something. I didn't want to say anything," Ami said with a head tilt. "I know a little bit about what was going on in Palm Beach, but I didn't know if he got shrunk by a god and had to stay that small." Ami reached out and scratched Archie's tiny head. "You *are* impossibly adorable now, you know."

"I am not *pocket-sized,* and I've always been impossibly adorable," he snapped imperiously at Ami, and turned his head to take aim at her fingers. She jerked her hand back. "No one did this to me. I could always change my size. I just... felt like garbage if you want to know the truth. So I shrank."

"Do you still feel like garbage?" Althea asked, joining us.

"I'm feeling fine now," Archie said. "And no, I don't feel like garbage anymore. But I did find it was easier to ride on Astra's shoulder when I was this size. If you must know, Miss Noseypants." Archie cast a scathingly offended glare at Ami, and he seemed to grow ever so slightly. "It's quite rude to talk about a gentleman's size, you know."

Ami glanced at me. "I thought he wasn't salty anymore?"

"Oh, that?" I half-smiled. "That lasted for about an hour. Maybe two. But yeah, that's over now."

"They just said I had to do my job; they didn't say I had to swallow all of my opinions like I was some sl—"

"Don't say it," Althea cut him off with a fierce look.

He looked back at her with his steely eyes, then relaxed back onto my shoulder.

"I'm sorry," Ami laughed. "I shouldn't have asked."

* * *

I MINGLED because it was a party, and I wasn't sure what I was supposed to do at a party other than mingle. So I watched and laughed and engaged in interesting conversations with the dozens of paranormals, gods, and humans in the know, hoping to get some kind of stunning revelation, some clear message.

But no.

It was just a Christmas party.

"Hi."

As I turned around, my eyes fell on Jason Bishop smiling at me. Jason—my morning running partner—looked like one of those guys who'd been on the cover of a teen magazine. He was tall, lean and muscular, and so clean-cut he practically squeaked when he walked. Though entirely human—with some possible latent supernatural ability since he was a middle school teacher, after all—Jason grew up in the most psychic town in the world and was no stranger to weirdness.

Like Greek gods throwing Christmas parties.

"Hey, yourself," I said with a smile back. The conversation I overheard Jason have with his mother played through my mind, and I did my best to shove it away.

Jason looked up above my head. "I wasn't sure if you knew, but you're standing directly under the mistletoe."

"I'm what?" I looked up, but of course, the mistletoe was right there. "I wouldn't worry about it. I'm not the kissing type."

Archie, tiny little owl that he was now, crawled under my hair and bit my earlobe. He hissed in my ear, "You know, if you say you're not the kissing type, then you're not the kissing type, but I should point out he waited a whole hour to come and say hello to you, and you've been under the kissing berries for all of a minute and a half!" The owl panted. "I do not want Aphrodite or Eros to show up tomorrow for *school the chosen one and her owl, episode two*! Stop it!"

I did my best not to wince from the pain as Archie released my ear.

"You're not, huh?" Jason's eyes crinkled, a bright, bright blue that seemed to glow against his pale skin. "Wanna come with me into the kitchen, then? It's a bit quieter in there. Or maybe out on the back porch?" He stepped forward and placed his arm lightly around me, and he smelled clean, in a fresh-out-of-bed kind of way. His smile was so crooked, so charming.

As much as I wanted to get away from the people and the noise, and as much as I knew I needed to talk to Jason, I wasn't sure what was supposed to happen to clarify my future had happened yet. "I don't think that's a good—"

"Have you ever been informed that you are the most infuriating woman on the planet? You have the social tact of a wild boar. Let's go," Archie said, and he nipped my ear again. "Go talk to him!"

I jumped and winced once more.

"So, yeah, I'll just go with you," I agreed with a smile, my eyes watery from the earlobe pain. "It's a little loud in here."

Jason guided me through the French doors leading out to the back porch, holding the door for me as I stepped out into the chill. He stepped away from me toward the rail, leaned against it, and looked up at the moon. Then he exhaled loudly. "Ami let me know a bit of what happened. You had one heck of a day," he said with a smile. "I thought Cassandra and the ghosts were complicated."

Archie jumped off my shoulder and skittered under the bushes. "Don't you go back there!" he muttered. "Stupid lizards. Always hiding." He stuck his head out and glared at me with a severe look. "I'm listening to everything. I can hunt and spy at the same time." Then his head disappeared.

I sighed.

Jason looked concerned. "Are you okay?"

"I just feel like everything in my life is complicated lately," I admitted. His face crumpled from the lighthearted, friendly smile, and he stared blankly at the ground. I felt awful. "Don't do that."

"Do what?" he asked quietly.

"Think that what I just said has to do with you." The tension between us was suddenly palpable, and I turned and sat down heavily on a chair. "I swear, for someone so capable with untold magic power, I'm not good at this at all." I looked up at him. "My whole day has been the universe taking me to task for pushing things away instinctively. Things that deserved a bit of brainpower to examine, a fair hearing but that I flatly refused to even entertain. The gods tried to show me that just because *I* have trust issues doesn't mean things in my life can't be trusted."

He raised his eyebrow. "You have trust issues?"

"Are you daft?" I asked, incredulous. "Yes, I

have trust issues! And thanks to my super-special place in the world, I got them all thrown at me for Christmas! Topped off with an Olympian Christmas party to *really* shove it all in my face! And it's clear I have to face it head on instead of backpacking through the Appalachian trail by myself—which is, frankly, what I really would prefer to be doing!" I glared at him resentfully and felt guilty doing it—none of this was Jason's fault.

Yes, I knew it was mine.

"Okay, okay! Sorry, I really didn't know!" Jason sat down slowly, his brow furrowed. "Wow. That must have been pretty tough."

"Yeah." I exhaled slowly. "Yeah."

We were quiet for a minute, the only sound the wind chimes on the porch.

"At the risk of getting my head bitten off again, why are you here with me?"

"Because you're sweet, you're funny, you're kind, and I like you." I leaned forward, clasping my hands together. "And I think you like me too. And I've been shutting you down because...oh, Jason, I don't know why I've been shutting you down. I'm just a mess." I put my head in my hands. "This must be the least romantic confession of attraction you've ever heard in your life."

"Hey." I felt his hands on mine. They gently pulled my hands away from my face and then released to tilt my head toward his. I raised my eyes to meet his gaze. "I do like you. I like you a lot." He smiled and brushed the hair from my face. "But we both know that this is a big step. There's a lot at stake here."

He was right, of course. I knew it. "Yes."

"But so much has been thrown at you recently. I don't want you to feel pressured to do something you don't want to do. So, if you don't want to…"

I waited.

He was going to finish that sentence, right?

I looked at him and saw he was waiting for a decision from me. I'm not sure that his eyes always looked that blue, but he was definitely looking at me like I was the most beautiful woman in the world. Jason was so close I could feel his breath on my mouth.

And if I leaned in just a little bit, I could kiss him.

My mouth went dry.

He leaned in toward me, his eyes still on mine.

I waited.

We were inches away.

This was the moment when I should have just leaned forward.

Or he should have leaned forward.

Turns out, we both did.

It was a chaste, gentle kiss. It felt like the next step in a natural progression from what we were to what we needed to be. It was soft and sweet, and the warmth of his lips felt good. It was a kiss that made me feel safe and happy and that I was exactly where I was supposed to be.

He stood up and offered his hand to me, and I let him pull me up from the chair.

"Astra, I don't want to screw this up," he said earnestly, his eyes staring deep into mine. "You're special like a demigod, an Oracle, a magical princess. I know I'm human, and this is... complicated," he admitted, a sad smile playing about his lips. He wrapped me in his arms and kissed me on the head. "But I don't want to screw this up."

"We'll go slow," I said with a shrug, leaning into his chest. "I've never done that before. In the military, there was never much time with—"

"Astra?"

"Yes?"

"I don't want to hear about your other relationships."

"That's just it," I told him, looking up. "They were barely relationships at—

"Astra?" he asked.

"Uh-huh?"

"I don't want to hear about your other men. Or women. Or whatever else may have come before," he explained. "At least not right now. Okay?"

"Okay," I said slowly, then looked up at him. "Thanks."

"You're welcome." He squeezed me. "But what for?"

"For understanding. For this," I said and kissed him. "For being my friend. For being a good listener. For being, well, you. Oh, and for not running for the hills when my owl attacked you."

"It's my pleasure," he said with a smile. Then the smile faded. "He's not going to do that anymore, is he?"

I shrugged. "Only time will tell, I suppose."

Jason laughed at that, and I thought about how much I liked hearing him laugh. "Well, I guess I'll get better at sprinting. So…what do you say to a glass of wine?"

"Or two?"

"Or three."

"Or four?"

"Or six?" He pulled back, his eyes twinkling. "I mean, there is a wine god at the party. So I suppose it would only be appropriate."

* * *

MY SISTERS AMI and Althea were ecstatic when Jason and I walked back into the party arm in arm. Emma, too, gave me the thumbs-up sign as she huddled with the mayor of Cassandra, the police captain, and Eddie Renzo. I looked around for Ayla, but my Aunt Gwennie told me she'd been sullen and angry all day and was holed up in her room.

Gods couldn't fix everything in one day.

As vampires, witches, elves, and gods sang Christmas carols in the living room, I marveled at how much had changed within me—and in my life—in just one day.

"I guess there are Christmas miracles," I said quietly.

Unfortunately, one day of joy, miracles, and change does not change the world, and my new relationship would be put to the test much sooner than I expected.

But that's a story for another time…

* * *

THANK YOU FOR READING!

I hope you enjoyed Owl About Yule. Please think about leaving a review! Astra, Archie and the whole Arden family continue their adventures in Book 6, Owl Melt with You.

KEEP UP WITH LEANNE LEEDS

Thanks so much for reading! I hope you liked it! Want to keep up with me?

Visit leanneleeds.com to:

Find all my books…

Sign up for my newsletter…

Like me on Facebook…

Follow me on Twitter…

Follow me on Instagram…

Thanks again for reading!

Leanne Leeds

FIND A TYPO? LET US KNOW!

Typos happen. It's sad, but true.

Though we go over the manuscript multiple times, have editors, have beta readers, and advance readers it's inevitable that determined typos and mistakes sometimes find their way into a published book.

Did you find one? If you did, think about reporting it on leanneleeds.com so we can get it corrected.

ARTIFICIAL INTELLIGENCE STATEMENT

Portions of this book were created with the assistance of AI tools used for editing, proofreading, and refining the text. However, the ideas, storyline, characters, and overall creative vision remain my own original work.

While some aspects of the cover image were generated using AI tools, it was done so under my creative direction and curation.

I want to acknowledge the use of these technologies as part of my creative process, while affirming that the essence of this work comes from my own imagination and effort.

Leanne Leeds

www.ingramcontent.com/pod-product-compliance
Lightning Source LLC
Chambersburg PA
CBHW021447240626
47153CB00001B/335